THE EARTH QUARTER

QUARTER

By
DAMON KNIGHT

ARMCHAIR FICTION
PO Box 4369, Medford, Oregon   97501-0168

"The Earth Quarter"

For more information about Armchair Books and products, visit our website at...

www.armchairfiction.com

Or email us at...

armchairfiction@yahoo.com

WELCOME TO THE QUARTER...

Human nature may not always be a good thing, but sometimes it can be as tough as rawhide—and when it came right down to it, death and hardship were no obstacle to the people of the Quarter...especially when they had the right incentive.

The Niroi permitted refugees from Earth to live in their cramped little ghetto conditionally: that they do so peacefully. But there would always be a few patriotic fanatics who wanted to disturb the peace...

FOR A COMPLETE SECOND NOVEL, TURN TO PAGE 69

CAST OF CHARACTERS

LASZLO CUDYK
The Quarter's leading citizen. He was old and tired—and responsible for keeping Harkway from getting into trouble!

JAMES HARKWAY
Young, handsome, and on a mission for what he believed was the best hope for the human race. Was he a fool, or a martyr?

CAPTAIN RACK
Not exactly an alien's best friend. He hated the Quarter, but he hated aliens even more—and he would bring the fight to them!

FERGUSON
He had the personality of a jackal, but he wielded more power in the Quarter than anyone else.

SEU MIN
Being Mayor of the Quarter had its advantages, and he wasn't afraid to take advantage of them to stay ahead of the game.

THE NIORI
They may have been six-limbed aliens with violet eyes, but they were smart—and they held man at bay in an intergalactic ghetto.

CHAPTER ONE

THE SUN had set half an hour before. Now, from the window of Laszlo Cudyk's garret, he could see how the alien city shone frost-blue against the black sky; the tall hive-shapes that no man would have built, glowing with their own light.

Nearer, the slender drunken shafts of lampposts marched toward him down the street, each with its prosaic yellow globe. Between them and all around, the darkness had gathered; darkness in angular shapes, the geometry of squalor.

Cudyk liked this view, for at night the blackness of the Earth Quarter seemed to merge with the black sky, as if one were a minor extension of the other—a fist of space held down to the surface of the planet. He could feel, then, that he was not alone, not isolated and forgotten; that some connection still existed across all the light-years of the galaxy between him and what he had lost.

And, again, the view depressed him; for at night the City seemed to press in upon the Quarter like the walls of a prison. The Quarter: sixteen square blocks, about the site of those of an Earth city, two thousand three hundred human beings of three races, four religions, eighteen nationalities; the only remnant of the human race nearer than Capella.

Cudyk felt the night breeze freshening. He glanced upward once at the frosty blaze of stars, then pulled his head back inside the window. He closed the shutters, turning to the lamp-lit table with its hopeless clutter of books, pipes and dusty miscellany.

Cudyk was a man of middle height, heavy in the shoulders and chest, blunt-featured, with a shock of graying black hair. He was fifty-five years old; he remembered Earth.

A drunk stumbled by in the street below, cursing monotonously to himself, paused to spit explosively into the gutter, and faded into the night.

Cudyk heard him without attention. He stood with his back to the window, looking at nothing, his square fingers fumbling automatically for pipe and tobacco. Why do I torture myself with that look out the window every night? he asked himself. It's a juvenile sentimentalism.

But he knew he would go on doing it.

Other noises drifted up to his window, faint with distance. They grew louder. Cudyk cocked his head suddenly, turned and threw open the shutters again. That had been a scream.

He could see nothing down the street; the trouble must be farther over, he thought, on Kwang-Chowfu or Washington. The noise swelled as he listened: the unintelligible wailing of a mob.

Footsteps clicked hurriedly up the stairs. Cudyk went to the door, made sure it was latched, and waited. There was a light tapping on the door.

"Who is it?" he said.

"Lee Far."

He unlatched the door and opened it. The little Chinese blinked at him, his upper lip drawn up over incisors like a rodent's. "Mr. Seu say please, you come." Without waiting for an answer, he turned and rapped his way down into darkness.

Cudyk picked up a jacket from a wall hook, and paused for a moment to glance at the locked drawer in which he kept an ancient .32 automatic and two full clips. He shook his head impatiently and went out.

Lee was waiting for him downstairs. When he saw Cudyk open the outer door, he set off down the street at a dogtrot.

Cudyk caught up with him at the corner of Athenai and Brasil. They turned right for two blocks to Washington, then left again. A block away, at Rossiya and Washington there was a small crowd of men struggling in the middle of the street. They didn't seem to be very active; as Cudyk and Lee approached; they saw that only a few were still fighting, and those without a great deal of spirit. The rest were moving aimlessly, some wiping their eyes, others bent almost double in paroxysms of sneezing. A few were motionless on the pavement.

Three slender Chinese were moving through the crowd. Each had a white surgeon's mask tied over his nose and mouth, and carried a plastic bag full of some dark substance, from which he took handfuls and flung them with a motion like a sower's. Cudyk could see now that the air around them was heavy with floating particles. As he watched, the last two fighters in the crowd each took a halfhearted swing at the other and then, coughing and sneezing, moved away in separate directions.

Lee took his sleeve for a moment. "Here, Mr. Cudyk."

Seu was standing in the doorway of Town Hall, his round-bellied bulk almost filling it. He saluted Cudyk with a lazy, humorous gesture of one fat hand.

"Hello, Min," Cudyk said. "You're efficient, as always. Pepper again?"

"Yes," said Mayor Seu Min. "I hate to waste it, but I don't think the water buckets would have been enough this time. This could have been a bad one."

"How did it start?"

"A couple of Russkies caught Jim Loong sneaking into Madame May's," the fat man said laconically. His shrewd eyes twinkled. "I'm glad you came down, Laszlo. I want you to meet an important visitor who arrived on the Kt-I'ith ship this afternoon." He turned slightly, and Cudyk saw that there was a man behind him in the doorway. "Mr. Harkway, may I present Mr. Laszlo Cudyk, one of our leading citizens? Mr. Cudyk, James Harkway, who is here on a mission from the Minority People's League."

Cudyk shook hands with the man, who had a pale,

scholarly face, not bad looking, with dark intense eyes. He was young, about thirty. Cudyk automatically classified him as second generation.

"Perhaps," said Seu, as if the notion had just occurred to him, "you would not mind taking over my duties as host for a short time, Laszlo? If Mr. Harkway would not object? This regrettable occurrence—"

"Of course," Cudyk said. Harkway nodded and smiled.

"Excellent." Seu edged past Cudyk, then turned and put a hand on his friend's arm, drawing him closer. "Take care of this fool," he said under his breath, "and for God's sake keep him away from the saloons. Rack is in town, too. I've got to make sure they don't meet." He smiled cheerfully at both of them and walked away. Lee Far, appearing from somewhere, trailed after him.

A young Chinese, with blood streaming brightly from a gash in his cheek, was stumbling past. Cudyk stepped away from the doorway, turned him around and pointed him down the street, to where Seu's young men were laying out the victims on the sidewalk and administering first aid.

Cudyk went back to Harkway. "I suppose Seu has found you a place to stay," he said.

"Yes," said Harkway. "He's putting me up in his home. Perhaps I'd better go there now—I don't want to be in the way."

"You won't be in the way," Cudyk told him. "What would you like to do?"

"Well, I'd like to meet a few people, if it isn't too late. Perhaps we could have a drink somewhere, where people meet—?" He glanced interrogatively down the street to an illuminated sign that announced in English and Russian: "THE LITTLE BEAR. Wines and Liquors."

"Not there," said Cudyk. "That's Russky headquarters, and I'm afraid they may be a little short-tempered right now.

The best place would be Chong Yin's tearoom, I think. That's just two blocks up, near Washington and Ceskosloven-sko."

"All right," said Harkway. He was still looking down the street. "Who is that girl?" he asked abruptly.

Cudyk glanced that way. The two M. D.'s, Moskowitz and Estrada, were on the scene, sorting out the most serious cases to be carted off to hospital, and so was a slender, dark-haired girl in nurse's uniform.

"That's Kathy Burgess," he said. "I'd introduce you, but now isn't the time. You'll probably meet her tomorrow."

"She's very pretty," said Harkway, and suffered himself to be led off up the street. "Married?"

"No. She was engaged to one of our young men, but her father broke it off."

"Oh?" said Harkway. After a moment: "Political differences?"

"Yes. The young man joined the activists. The father is a conservative."

"That's very interesting," said Harkway. After a moment he asked, "Do you have many of those here?"

"Activists or conservatives? Or pretty girls?"

"I meant conservatives," said Harkway, coloring slightly. "I know the activist movement is strong here—that's why I was sent. We consider them dangerous in the extreme."

"So do I," said Cudyk. "No, there aren't many conservatives. Burgess is the only real fanatic. If you meet him, by the way, you must make certain allowances."

Harkway nodded thoughtfully. "Cracked on the subject?"

"You could put it that way," Cudyk told him. "He has convinced himself, in his conscious mind at least, that we are the dominant species on this planet; that the Niori are our social and economic inferiors. He won't tolerate any suggestion that it isn't so."

Harkway nodded again, looking very solemn. "A tragedy," he said. "But understandable, of course. Some of the older people simply can't adjust to the reality of our position in the galaxy."

"Not many people actually like it," said Cudyk.

Harkway looked at him thoughtfully. He said, "Mr. Cudyk, I don't want you to take this as a complaint, but I've gathered the impression that you're not in sympathy with the Minority People's League."

"No," said Cudyk.

"May I ask what your political viewpoint is?"

"I'm neutral," said Cudyk. "Apolitical."

Harkway said politely, "I hope you won't take offense if I ask why? It's evident, even to me, that you're a man of intelligence and ability."

Everything is evident to you, Cudyk thought wearily, except what you don't want to see. He said, "I don't believe our particular Humpty Dumpty can be put back together again, Mr. Harkway."

Harkway looked at him intently, but said nothing. He glanced at the signboard over the lighted windows they were approaching. "Is this the place?"

"Yes."

Harkway continued to look at the sign. Above the English "CHONG YIN'S TEA ROOM", and the Chinese characters, was a legend that read:

ſ‖ \ᒪ/ᒪᒍ 'ᒥ\‖ ᕋᕋᕋ\ᒥ\

"That's a curious alphabet," he said.

"It's a very efficient one," Cudyk told him. "It's based on the design of an X in a rectangle—like this." He traced it with his finger on the wall. "Counting each arm of the cross as one stroke, there are eight strokes in the figure. Using only two strokes to a letter, there are twenty-eight possible combinations. They use the sixteen most graceful ones, and add twenty-seven three-stroke letters to bring it up to forty-three, one for each sound in their language. The written language is completely phonetic, therefore. But there are only eight keys on a Niori typewriter."

He looked at Harkway. "It's also perfectly legible: no letter looks too much like any other letter. And it has a certain beauty, don't you think?" He paused. "Hasn't it struck you, Mr. Harkway, that anything our hosts do is likely to be a little more sensible and more sensitive than the human equivalent?"

"I come from Reg Otay," said Harkway. "They don't have any visual arts or any written language there. But I see what you mean. What does the sign say—the same thing as the English?"

"No. It says, 'Yungiwo Ren Trakru Rith.' 'Trakru rith' is Niori for 'hospitality house'—it's what they call anything that we would call tea room, or restaurant, or beer garden."

"And 'Yungiwo Ren'?"

"That's their version of 'Chung kuo jen'*—the Chinese for 'Chinese.' At first they called us all that, because most of the original immigrants were from China; but they've got over it now—they found out some of us didn't like it."

Cudyk opened the door. A few aliens were sitting at the round tables in the big outer room. Cudyk watched Harkway's face, and saw his eyes widen with shock. The Niori were something to see, the first time.

They were tall and erect, and their anatomy was not even remotely like man's. They had six limbs each, two for walking, four for manipulation. Their bodies were covered by a pale, horny integument, which grew in irregular sections

----

*Pronounced "jung guo ren".

so that you could tell the age of a Niori by the width of the growth-areas between the plates of his armor. But you saw none of those things at first. You saw the two glowing violet eyes, set wide apart in a helmet-shaped head, and the startlingly beautiful markings on the smooth shell of the face—blue on pale cream, like an ancient porcelain tile. And you saw the crest—a curved, lucent shape that even in a lighted room glowed with its own frost-blue. No Niori ever walked in darkness.

Cudyk guided Harkway toward the door at the far end of the room. "We'll see who's in the back room," he said. "There is usually a small gathering at this hour."

The inner room was more brightly lit than the other. Down the center, in front of a row of empty booths, was a long table. Three men sat at one end of it, with teacups and a bowl of lichee nuts between them. They looked up as Cudyk and Harkway came in.

"Gentlemen," said Cudyk, "may I present Mr. Harkway, who is here on a mission from the Minority People's League? Mr. Burgess, Father Exarkos, Mr. Ferguson."

The three shook hands with Harkway, Father Exarkos smiling pleasantly, the other two with more guarded expressions. The priest was in his fifties, grey-haired, hollow-templed, with high orbital ridges and a square, mobile mouth. He said, in English oddly accented by a mixture of French and Greek, "Please sit down, both of you... I understand that your first evening here has been not too pleasant, Mr. Harkway. I hope the rest of your stay will be more so."

Burgess snorted, not quite loudly enough to be deliberately rude. His face had a pleasant, even a handsome cast except for the expression of petulance he was now wearing. He was a few years younger than the priest: a big-boned, big-featured man whose slightly curved back and hollowed cheeks showed that he had lost bulk since his prime.

Ferguson's pale face was expressive but completely controlled. The gambler's eyes were narrow and unreadable, the lips and the long muscles of the jaw showing nothing more than surface emotion. He asked politely, "Planning to stay long, Mr. Harkway?"

"That all depends, Mr. Ferguson, on—to be blunt, on what sort of a reception I get. I won't try to conceal from you the fact that my role here is that of a political propagandist. I want to convince as many people as I can that the Minority People's movement is the best hope of the human race. If I can find that there's some chance of succeeding, I'll stay as long as necessary. If not—"

"I'm afraid we won't be seeing much of you, in that case, Mr. Harkway," said Burgess. His tone was scrupulously correct, but his nostrils were quivering with repressed indignation.

"What makes you say that, Mr. Burgess?" Harkway asked, turning his intent, serious gaze on the older man.

"Your program, as I understand it," said Burgess, "aims at putting humanity on an equal basis with various assorted races of lizards, beetles and other vermin. I don't think you will find much sympathy for that program here, sir."

"I'm glad to say that, through no fault of your own, you're mistaken," said Harkway, smiling slightly. "I think you're referring to the program of the right wing of the League, which was dominant for the last several years. It's true that for that period, the M. P. L.'s line was to work for the gradual integration of human beings—and other repressed races—into the society of the planets on which they live. But that's all done with now. The left wing, to which I belong, has won a decisive victory at the League elections.

"Our program," Harkway continued earnestly, "rejects the doctrine of assimilation as a biological and cultural absurdity. What we propose to do, and with sufficient help will do, is to return humanity to its homeland—to reconstitute Earth as an autonomous, civilized member of the galactic entity. We realize, of course, that this is a gigantic undertaking, and that much aid will be required from the other races of the galaxy... Were you about to say something, Mr. Burgess?"

Burgess said bitterly, "What you mean, in plain words, Mr. Harkway, is that you think we all ought to go home—dissolve Earth's galactic empire—give it all back to the natives. I don't think you'll find much support for *that*, either."

Harkway bit his lip, and cast a glance at Cudyk that seemed to say, You warned me, but I forgot. He turned to Ferguson, who was smiling around his cigar as blandly as if nothing out of the way had been said. "What is your view, Mr. Ferguson?"

Ferguson waved his cigar amiably. "You'll have to count me out, Mr. Harkway. I'm doing okay as things are—I have no reason to want any changes."

Harkway turned to the little priest. "And you, Father Exarkos?"

The Greek shrugged and smiled. "I wish you all the luck in the universe, sincerely," he said. "But I am afraid I believe that no material methods can rescue man from his dilemma."

"If I've given any offense," said Burgess suddenly, "I can leave."

Harkway stared at him for a moment, gears almost visibly slipping in his head. Then he said, "Of course not, Mr. Burgess, please don't think that for a moment. I respect your views—"

Burgess looked around him with a wounded expression. "I know," he said with difficulty, "that I am in a minority—here—"

Father Exarkos put a hand on his arm and murmured something. Harkway leaned forward impulsively across the table and said, "Mr. Burgess, I've traveled a long way in the hope of discussing these problems with men of intelligence and standing in their community, like yourself. I hope you'll stay and give me the benefit of your experience. I shall be very much the loser if you don't."

Burgess was visibly struggling with his emotions. He stood up and said, "No—no—not tonight. I'm upset. Please excuse me." Head bowed, he walked out of the room.

There was a short silence. "Did I do the wrong thing?" asked Harkway.

"No, no," said Father Exarkos. "It was not your fault— there was nothing you could do. You must excuse him. He is a good man, but he has suffered too much. Since his wife died—of a disease contracted during one of the Famines, you understand—he has not been himself."

Harkway nodded, looking both older and more human than he had a moment before. "If we can only turn back the clock," he said. "Put Humpty Dumpty together again, as you expressed it, Mr. Cudyk." He smiled apologetically at them. "I won't harangue you any more tonight—I'll save that for the meeting tomorrow. But I hope that some of you will come to see it my way."

Father Exarkos' eyebrows lifted. "You are planning to hold a public meeting tomorrow?"

"Yes. There's some difficulty about space—Mayor Seu tells me that the town hall is already booked for the next three days—but I'm confident that I can find some suitable place. If necessary, I'll make it an open-air meeting."

Rack, thought Cudyk. Rack usually stays in town for only two or three days at a time. Seu is trying to keep Harkway under cover until he leaves. It won't work.

Out of the corner of his eye he saw a dark shape in the doorway, and his first thought was that Burgess had come back. But it was not Burgess. It was a squat, bandy-legged man with huge shoulders and arms, wearing a leather jacket and a limp military cap. Cudyk sat perfectly still, warning Exarkos with his eyes.

The squat man walked casually up the table, nodding almost imperceptibly to Ferguson. He ignored the others, except the M. P. L. man. "Your name Harkway?" he asked. He pronounced it with the flat Boston "a": "Haakway".

"That's right," said Harkway.

"Got a message for you," said the squat man. "From Captain Lawrence Rack, United Uth Space Navy."

"The Earth Space Navy was dissolved twenty years ago," said Harkway.

The squat man sighed. "You wanna heah the message or don't you?" he asked.

"Go ahead," said Harkway. His nostrils were pale, and a muscle stood out at the side of his jaw.

"Heah it is. You're plannin' to hold a meetin' of the vehmin lovehs society, right?"

As Harkway began to reply, the squat man leaned across the table and backhanded him across the mouth, knocking him sideways out of his chair.

"Don't," said the squat man. He turned and strolled out.

Cudyk and Ferguson helped Harkway up. The man's eyes were staring wildly out of his pale face, and a thin trickle of blood was running from a pulped lip. "Who was that man?" he asked in a whisper.

"His name is Monk," said Cudyk. "At least that is the only name he has been known to answer to. He is one of Rack's lieutenants—Rack, as you probably know, is the leader of the activists in this sector. Mr. Harkway, I'm sorry this happened. But I advise you to wait for a week or so before you hold your meeting. There is no question of courage involved. It would be suicide."

Harkway looked at him blindly. "The meeting will be held as planned," he said, and walked out, stiff-legged.

Ferguson shook his head, laughed, and shook his head again. Cudyk exchanged a hopeless glance with Father Exarkos, and then followed Harkway out of the room.

CHAPTER TWO

THE SHOP was empty except for young Nick Pappageorge, dozing behind the long counter, and the pale morning sunlight that streamed through the plastic window. Most of the counter was in shadow, but stray fingers of light picked out gem trays here and there, turning them into minuscule galaxies of frosty brilliance.

Two Niori, walking arm in arm, paused in front of the window display, then went on. Two human youngsters raced by, shouting. Cudyk caught only a glimpse of them through the pierced screen that closed off the back of his shop, but he recognized them by their voices: Red Gorciak and Stan Eleftheris.

There were few children now, and they were growing up wild. Cudyk wondered briefly what it must be like to be a child born into this microcosm, knowing no other. He dismissed the thought; it was simply one more thing about which there was no use to worry.

Cudyk hadn't spoken to anyone that morning, but he knew approximately what was happening. Seu would have been busy most of the night, covering up traces of last evening's riot. Now, probably, he was explaining it away to Zydh Oran, the Niori Outgroup Commissioner. Harkway was in preparations for his meeting—another thing for Seu to worry about when he got through cleaning up the last mess.

Barring miracles today was going to be very bad.

Seu came in, moving quickly. He walked directly to the rear of the shop. His normally bland face looked worried, and there were beads of sweat on his wide forehead, although the morning was cool.

"Sit down," said Cudyk. "You've seen Zydh Oran?"

Seu made a dismissing gesture. "Nothing. Not pleasant, but nothing. The same as usual—he tells me what happened, I deny it. He knows, but under their laws he can't do anything."

"Someday it will be bad," said Cudyk.

"Yes. Someday. Laszlo—you've got to do something about Harkway. Otherwise he's going to be killed tonight, and there will be a stink from here to Sirius. I had to tell him he could use Town Hall—he was all ready to hold a torch-light meeting in the streets."

"I tried," said Cudyk.

"Try again. Please. Your ethnic background is closer to his than mine. He respects you, I think. Perhaps he's even read some of your books. If anyone can persuade him, you can."

"What did he say when you talked to him?"

"An ox. A brain made of soap and granite. He says it is a matter of principle. I knew then that I could do nothing. When an Anglo-Saxon talks about his principles, you may as well go home. He won't accept a weapon, he won't postpone the meeting. I think he wants to be a martyr."

Cudyk frowned. "Maybe he does. Have you seen Rack?"

"No. Ferguson pretends not to know where he is."

"That's rather odd. What is his motive, do you think?"

Seu said, "Basically, he is afraid of Rack. He cooperates with him—they use each other—but you know that it's not a marriage of minds. He knows that Rack is stronger than he is, because he is only an amoral egotist, and Rack is a fanatic. I think he believes this business may be Rack's downfall, and he would like that."

He stood up. "I have to go. Will you do it?"

"Yes."

"Good. Let me know." Seu walked out, as hastily as he had entered.

Nick Pappageorge had roused himself and was polishing a tall, fluted silver vase. Cudyk said, "Nick, go and find out where Mr. Harkway is. If he isn't busy, ask him if he'll do me the favor of dropping around to see me. Otherwise, just come back and tell me where he is; I'll go to him."

Nick said, "Sure, Mr. Cudyk," and went out.

Cudyk stared at the tray of unsorted gems on the desk before him. He stirred them with his forefinger, separating out an emerald, two aquamarines, a large turquoise and a star sapphire. That was all he had had to begin with—his dead wife's jewels, carried half across Europe when a loaf of bread was worth more than all the gemstones in the world. The sapphire had bought his passage on the alien ship; the others had been his original stock-in-trade, first at the refugee center on Alfhal, then here on Palumbar. Now he was a prosperous importer, with a business that netted him the equivalent of ten thousand pounds a year.

But the wealth was ashes; he would have traded all of it for one loaf of bread, eaten in peace, on an Earth that had not sunk back to barbarism.

Momentum, he told himself. Momentum and a remnant of curiosity. Those are the only reasons I can think of why I do not blowout my brains. I wonder what keeps the others from it? Seu? Chong Yin? I don't know. Burgess has his fantasy, though it cracks now and then. Ferguson has the sensibility of a jackal. Rack, as Seu said, is a fanatic. But why do the rest of them keep on? For what?

The doorway darkened again as Harkway came in, followed by Nick. Nick gestured toward the rear of the shop, and Harkway advanced, smiling. His lower lip was stained by a purple substance with a glossy surface.

Cudyk greeted him and offered him a chair. "It was good of you to come over," he said. "I hope I didn't interrupt your work."

Harkway grinned stiffly. "No. I was just finishing lunch when your boy found me. I have nothing more to do until this evening."

Cudyk looked at him. "Got to the hospital after all, I see."

"Yes. Dr. Moskowitz fixed me up nicely."

Cudyk had been asking himself why the M. P. L. man looked so cheerful. Now he thought he understood.

"And Miss Burgess?" he asked.

"Yes," said Harkway, looking embarrassed. He paused. "She's—an exquisite person, Mr. Cudyk."

Cudyk clasped his square hands together, elbows on the arms of his chair. He said, "Forgive me; I'm going to be personal. Am I right in saying that you now feel more than casually interested in Miss Burgess?"

He added, "Please. I have a reason for asking."

Harkway's expression was guarded. "Yes; that's true."

"Do you think she may feel similarly towards you?"

Harkway paused. "I think so. I hope so. Why, Mr. Cudyk?"

"Mr. Harkway, I will be very blunt. Miss Burgess has already lost one lover through no fault of her own, and the experience has not been good for her. She is, as you say, exquisite—she has a beautiful, but not a strong personality. Do you think it is fair for you to give her another such experience, even if the attachment is not fully formed, by allowing yourself to be killed this evening?"

Harkway leaned back in his chair. "Oh," he said, "That's it." He grinned. "I thought you were going to point out that her father broke off the last affair because of the man's politics. If you had, I was going to tell you that Mr. Burgess looked me up this morning and apologized for his attitude yesterday, and breaking down and so on. He's very decent, you know. We're getting along very well."

He paused. "About this other matter," he said seriously, "I'm grateful for your interest, but—I'm afraid I can't concede the validity of your argument." He made an impatient gesture. "I'm not trying to sound noble, but this business is more important than my personal life. That's all, I'm afraid. I'm sorry."

Another fanatic, Cudyk thought. A liberal fanatic. I have seen all kinds, now. He said, "I have one more argument to try. Has Seu explained to you how precarious our position is here on Palumbar?"

"He spoke of it."

"The Niori accepted this one small colony with grave misgivings. Every act of violence that occurs here weakens our position, because it furnishes ammunition for a group, which already wants to expel us. Do you understand?"

There was pain in Harkway's eyes. "Mr. Cudyk, it's the same all over the galaxy, wherever these pitifully tiny out groups exist. My group is trying to attack that problem on a galaxy-wide scale. I don't say we'll succeed, and I grant you the right to doubt that our program is the right one. But we've got to try. Among other things, we've got to clean out the activists, for just the reason you mention. And—pardon me for stressing the obvious—but it's Captain Rack who will be responsible for this particular act of violence if it occurs, not myself."

"And you think that your death at his hands would be a stronger argument than a peaceful meeting, is that it?"

Harkway shook his head ruefully. "I don't know that I have that much courage, Mr. Cudyk. I'm hoping that nothing will happen to me. But I know that the League's prestige here would be enormously hurt if I let Rack bluff me down." He stood up. "You'll be at the meeting?"

"I'm afraid so." Cudyk stood and offered his hand. "The best of luck."

He watched the young man go, feeling very old and tired. He had known it would be this way; he had only tried for Seu's sake. Now he was involved; he had allowed himself to feel the tug of love and pity toward still another lost soul. Such bonds were destructive—they turned the heart brittle and weathered it away, bit by bit.

The assembly hall was well filled, although Harkway had made no special effort to advertise the meeting. He had known, Cudyk thought, that Rack's threat would be more than sufficient. The youngster was not stupid.

There were no women or children. Ferguson was there, and a large contingent of his employees—gamblers, pimps, waiters and strong-arm men—as well as most of the Russian population. All but a few of the Chinese had stayed away, as had Burgess. But a number of men whom Cudyk knew to have M. P. L. leanings, and an even larger number of neutrals, were there. The audience was about evenly divided, for and against Harkway. If he somehow came through this alive, it was just possible that he could swing the Quarter his way. A futile victory; but of course Harkway did not believe that.

There was a murmur and a shuffle of feet as Rack entered with three other men—Monk, the one called Spider, and young Tom De Grasse, who had once been engaged to Kathy Burgess. The sound dropped almost to stillness for a few moments after the four men took seats at the side of the hall, then rose again to a steady rumble. Harkway and Seu had not yet appeared.

Cudyk saw the man to his right getting up, moving away; he turned in time to see Seu wedge himself through a gap in the line of chairs and sit down in the vacated place.

The fat man's face was blandly expressionless, but Cudyk

knew that something had happened. "What is it?" he asked.

Seu's lips barely moved. He looked past Cudyk, inspecting the crowd with polite interest. "I had him kidnapped," he said happily. "He's tied up, in a safe place. There won't be any meeting today."

Seu had been seen. Someone a few rows ahead called, "Where's Harkway, Mayor?"

"I don't know," Seu said blandly. "He told me he would meet me here—said he had an errand to do. Probably he's on his way now."

Under cover of the ensuing murmur, he turned to Cudyk again. "I didn't want to do it," he said. "It will mean trouble, sooner or later; maybe almost as much trouble as if Harkway had been killed. But I had to make a choice. Do you think I did the right thing, Laszlo?"

"Yes," said Cudyk, "except that I wish you had told me earlier."

Seu smiled, his heavy face becoming for that instant open and confiding. "If I had, you wouldn't have been so sincere when you talked to Harkway."

Cudyk smiled in spite of himself. He relaxed in his chair, savoring the relief that had come when he'd learned that Harkway was not going to die. The tension built up, day by day, almost imperceptibly, and it was a rare, fleeting pleasure when something happened to lower it.

He saw the mayor looking at his watch. The crowd was growing restless: in a few more minutes Seu would get up and announce that the meeting was cancelled. Then it would be all over.

Seu was rising when a new wave of sound traveled over the audience. Out of the corner of his eye Cudyk saw men turning, standing up to see over the heads of their neighbors. Seu spoke a single, sharp word, and his hand tightened on the back of his chair.

Cudyk stood. Someone was coming down the center aisle of the room, but he couldn't see who it was.

Those who had stood earlier were sitting down now. Down the aisle, looking straight ahead, with a bruised jaw and a bloody scratch running from cheekbone to chin, came James Harkway.

He mounted the platform, rested both hands on the low speaker's stand, and turned his glance across the audience, once, from side to side. There was a collective scraping of chairs and clearing of throats, then complete stillness. Harkway said:

"My friends—and enemies."

Subdued laughter rippled across the room.

"A few of my enemies didn't want me to hold this meeting," said Harkway, "Some of my friends felt the same way. In fact, it seemed that *nobody* wanted this meeting to take place. But here you all are, just the same. And here I am."

He straightened. "Why is that, I wonder? Perhaps because regardless of our differences, we're all in the same boat—in a lifeboat." He nodded gravely. "Yes, we're all in a lifeboat—all of us together, to live or die, and we don't know which way to turn for the nearest land that will give us harbor.

"Which way shall we turn to find a safe landing? To find peace and honor for ourselves and our children? To find safety, to find happiness?"

He spread his arms. "There are a million directions we could follow. There are all the planets in the galaxy! But everywhere we turn, we find alien soil, alien cultures, and alien people. Everywhere except in one direction only.

"Our ship—our own planet, Earth—is foundering, is sinking, that's true. But it *hasn't—yet—sunk*. There's still a chance that we can turn back, make Earth what it was, and

24

then, from there—go on! Go on, until we've made a greater
Earth, a stronger, happier, more peaceful Earth—till we can
take our place with pride in the galaxy, and hold up our heads
with any other race that lives."

He had captured only half their attention, and he knew it.
They were watching him, listening to what he said, but the
heads of the audience were turned slightly, like the heads of
plants under a solar tropism, toward the side of the chamber
where Rack and his men sat.

Harkway said, "We all know that the Earth's technical
civilization is smashed—broken like an eggshell. By
ourselves, we could never put it back together. And if we do
nothing, no one else is going to put it back together for us.
But suppose we went to the other races in the galaxy, and
said—"

A baritone voice broke in quietly, *"We'll sell our souls to you,
if you'll kindly give us a few machines!"*

Rack stood up—tall, muscular, lean, with deep hollows
under his cheekbones, red-grey hair falling over his forehead
under the visor of his cap. His short leather jacket was
thrown over his shoulders like a cloak. His narrow features
were grey and cold, the mouth a straight, hard line. He said,
"That's what you want us to tell the vermin, isn't it, Mr.
Harkway?"

Harkway seemed to settle himself like a boxer. He said
clearly, "The intelligent races of the galaxy are not devils and
do not want our souls, Mr. Rack."

Rack ignored the "Mr." He said, "But they'd want certain
assurances from us, in return for their help, wouldn't they,
Mr. Harkway?"

"Certainly," said Harkway. "Assurances that no sane man
would refuse them. Assurances, for example, that there
would be no repetition of the Altair Incident—when a

handful of maniacs in two ships murdered thousands of peaceful galactic citizens without the slightest provocation. Perhaps you remember that, Mr. Rack; perhaps you were there."

"I was there," said Rack casually. "About five hundred thousand vermin were squashed. We would have done a better job, but we ran out of supplies. Some day we'll exterminate them all, and then there'll be a universe fit for men to live in. Meanwhile—" he glanced at the audience—"we're going to build. We're building now. Not with the vermin's permission, under the vermin's eye. In secret. On a planet they'll never find until our ships spurt out from it like milt from a fish. And when that day comes, we'll squash them down to the last tentacle and the last claw."

"Are you finished?" asked Harkway. He was quivering with controlled rage.

"Yes, I'm finished," said Rack wearily. "So are you. You're a traitor, Harkway, the most miserable kind of a crawling, dirt-eating traitor the human race ever produced. Get down off the platform."

Harkway said to the audience, "I came here to try to persuade you to my way of thinking—to ask you to consider the arguments and decide for yourselves. This man wants to settle the question by prejudice and force. Which of us is best entitled to the name 'human?' If you listen to him, can you blame the Niori if they decide to end even this tiny foothold they've given you on their planet? Would you live in a universe drenched with blood?"

Rack said quietly, "Monk."

The squat man stood up, smiling. He took a clasp knife out of his pocket, opened it, and started up the side of the room.

In the dead stillness, another voice said, "No!"

It was, Cudyk saw with shock, Tom De Grasse. The

26

youngster was up, moving past Rack—who made no move to stop him, did not even change expression—past the squat man, turning a yard beyond, almost at the front of the room. His square, almost childish face was tight with strain. There was a pistol in one big hand.

Cudyk felt something awaken in him which blossomed only at moments like this, when one of his fellow men did something particularly puzzling: the root, slain but still quasi-living, of the thing that had once been his central drive and his trademark in the world—his insatiable, probing, warmly intelligent curiosity about the motives of men.

On the surface, this action of De Grasse's was baldly impossible. He was committed to Rack's cause twice over, by conviction and by the shearing away of every other tie; and still more important, he worshipped Rack himself with the devotion that only fanatics can inspire. It was as if Peter had defied Christ.

The three men stood motionless for what seemed a long time. Monk, halted with his weight on one foot, faced De Grasse with his knife hand slightly extended, thumb on the blade. He was visibly tense, waiting for a word from Rack. But Rack stood as if he had forgotten time and space, staring bemused over Monk's shoulder at De Grasse. The fourth man, Spider—bones and gristle, with a corpse-growth of grey-white hair—stood up slowly. Rack put a hand on his shoulder and pressed him down again.

Cudyk thought: Kathy Burgess.

It was the only answer. De Grasse knew, of course, everything that had passed between Harkway and the girl.

CHAPTER THREE

There was no privacy worth mentioning in the Quarter. Pressed in this narrow ghetto, every man swam in the effluvium of every other man's emotions. And De Grasse was willing, apparently, to give up everything that mattered to him, to save Kathy Burgess pain.

It said something for the breed, Cudyk thought—not enough, never enough, for you saw it only in pinpoint flashes, the noble individual who was a part of the bestial mob—but a light in the darkness, nevertheless.

Finally Rack spoke. "You, Tom?"

The youngster's eyes showed sudden pain. But he said, "I mean it, Captain."

There was a slow movement out from that side of the room, men inching away, crowding against their neighbors.

Rack was still looking past Monk's shoulder, into De Grasse's face. He said:

"All right."

He turned, still wearing the same frozen expression, and walked down the side of the room, toward the exit. Monk threw a glance of pure incredulity over his shoulder, glanced back at De Grasse, and then followed. Spider scrambled after.

De Grasse relaxed slowly, as if by conscious effort. He put away his gun, hesitated a moment, and walked slowly out after the others. His wide shoulders were slumped.

Then there was the scraping of chairs and boot-soles and a rising beehive hum as the audience stood up and began to move out. Harkway made no effort to call them back.

Cudyk, moving toward the exit with the rest, had much to think about. He had seen not only De Grasse's will, but Rack's, part against the knife of human sympathy. And that was a thing he had never expected to see.

"Times like this," said Ferguson, narrowing his grey snake's eyes in a smile, "I almost believe in God."

Father Exarkos smiled courteously and said nothing. He

and Cudyk had been sitting in the back room of Chong Yin's since a half-hour after the meeting. Seu had been with them earlier, but had left. A little after twelve, Ferguson had strolled in and joined them.

"I mean it," said Ferguson, laughing a little. "There was Harkway, sticking his neck out, and there was little De Grasse standing in the way. And Rack backed down." He shook his head, still smiling. "Rack backed down. Now how would you explain that, gentlemen?"

It was necessary to put up with the gambler, who wielded more power in the Quarter than anyone else, even Seu; but sometimes Cudyk found himself dropping his usual attitude of detached interest in favor of speculations about the specific variety of horrible fate which Ferguson would most probably meet.

He was particularly irritating tonight, because Cudyk was forced to agree with him. Cudyk had still not solved the riddle of Rack's failure to finish what he had started.

It was conceivable that De Grasse should have acted as he did for reasons of sentiment; but to apply the same motive to Rack was simply not possible. The man had emotions, certainly, but they were all channeled into one direction: the destiny of the human race and of Lawrence Rack. De Grasse was at an age when the strongest emotions were volatile, when conversions were made, when a man could plan an assassination one day and enter a monastery the next. But Rack was fixed and aimed, like a cannon.

Ferguson was saying, "He must be going soft. Going soft—old Rack. Unless it's the hand of God. What's your opinion, Father?"

The priest said blandly, "Mr. Ferguson, since I have come to live upon this planet, my opinions have changed about many things. I no longer believe that either God, or man, is quite as simple as I once thought. We were too small in our thoughts, before—our understanding of temporal things was bounded by the frontiers of Earth, and of eternal things by the little sky we could see from our windows.

"Before, I think I would have tried to answer your question. I would have said that I think Captain Rack was moved by—a sudden access of human feeling—or I would have said that I think Captain Rack was touched by the finger of God. Perhaps I would have hesitated to say that, because even then I did not believe that God interferes with the small sins of men like Captain Rack. Or the small sins of anybody, for that matter."

Ferguson grinned. "Well, Father, that's the best excuse for an answer I ever heard, anyway." He dragged on his cigar, narrowing his eyes and pursing his lips, as if the cigar were a tube through which his brains were being sucked. "In other words," he said, "you don't think the big blowup back home was a judgment on us for our sins. You think it was a good thing, only more people should have got out the way we did. That right?"

"Oh, no," said Father Exarkos. "I believe that the Famines and the Collapse were a judgment of God. I have heard many theories about the causes of the Collapse, but I have not heard one which does not come back, in the end, to a condemnation of man's folly, cruelty, and blindness."

"Well," said Ferguson, "excuse me, Father, but if you believe that way, what are you doing here? Back there—" he jerked his head, as if Earth was some little distance behind his right shoulder—"people are living like animals. Chicago, where I come from, is just a stone jungle, with a few beast-like scavengers prowling around in it. If the dirt and disease don't get you, some bandit will split your head open, or you'll run into a wolf or some other hungry animal. If none of those things happen, you can expect to live to the ripe old age of forty, and then you'll be glad to die."

He had stopped smiling. Ferguson, Cudyk realized, was describing his own personal hell. He went on, "Now, if you want to call that a judgment, I won't argue with you. But if that's what you believe, why aren't you back there taking it with the rest of them?"

He really wanted to know, Cudyk thought. He had begun by trying to bait the priest, but now he was serious. It was odd to think of Ferguson having trouble with his conscience, but Cudyk was not really surprised. The most moralistic men he had ever known had been gangsters of Ferguson's type; whereas the few really good men he had known, Father Exarkos among them, had seemed as blithely unaware of their consciences as of their healthy livers.

The priest said, soberly, "Mr. Ferguson, I believe that we also are being punished. Perhaps we more than others. The Mexican peon, the Indian fellah, the peasant of China or Greece, lives very much as his father did before him; he scarcely has reason to know that judgment has fallen upon Earth. But I think that no inhabitant of the Quarter can forget it for so much as an hour."

Ferguson stared at him, then grunted and squashed out his cigar. He stood up. "I'll be getting along home," he said. "Good night." He walked out.

Cudyk and Exarkos sat for a while longer, talking quietly, and then left together. The streets were empty. Behind them and to their left as they walked to the corner, the ghostly blue of the Niori beehives shone above the dark human buildings.

The priest lived in a small second-floor apartment near the corner of Brasil and Athenai, alone since his wife had died ten years before. Cudyk had only to go straight across Ceskoslovensko, but he walked down toward Brasil with his friend.

Near the corner, Cudyk saw a dark form sprawled in a doorway. "One of your congregation, Astereos?" he asked.

"It is probable," said the priest resignedly. "Steve Chrisudis has been drinking heavily again this past week; also the two Moulios brothers."

He stepped over and turned the man's face up to the light.

The face was bloody and broken, the eyes sightless. It was Harkway. He had been dead long enough to grow cold.

CHAPTER FOUR

ONE QUESTION of Harkway's kept coming back to Cudyk. "Would you live in a universe drenched with blood?"

Rack would, of course; for others there was a tragic dilemma. For them, the race had come to the end of a road that had its beginning in prehistory. Every step of progress on that way had been accomplished by bloodshed, and yet the goal had always been a world at peace. It had been possible to live with the paradox when the road still seemed endless: before the first Earth starships discovered that humanity was not alone in the universe.

Human beings were like a fragile crystalline structure, enduring until the first touch of air; or like a cyst that withers when it is cut open. The winds of the universe blew around them now, and there was no way to escape from their own nature.

The way forward was the way back; the way back was the way forward.

There was no peace except the peace of surrender and death. There was no victory except the victory of chaos.

As the priest had remarked, there were many theories about the Collapse. It was said that the economy of Earth had been wrecked by interstellar imports; it was said that the rusts and blights that had devastated Earth's fields were of alien origin; it was said that the disbanding of the Space Navy, after the Altair Incident, had broken Earth's spirit. It was said that the emigrations, both before and after the Famines, had bled away too much of the trained manpower that was Earth's life-blood.

The clear fact was that the human race was finished: dying like Neanderthal faced by Cro-Magnon; dying like the hairy Ainu among the Japanese. It was true that hundreds of millions of people lived on Earth much as they had done before, tilling their fields, digging stones from the ground, laboring over the handicrafts which sustained the men of the Quarter in their exile.

Humanity had passed through such dark ages before.

But now there was no way to go except downward.

If the exiles in their ghettoes, on a hundred planets of the galaxy; were the lopped-off head of the race, then the ferment of theories, plans, and policies that swirled through them stood for the last fitful fantasies in the brain of a guillotined man.

And on Earth, the prelates, the robber barons, the petty princes were ganglia: performing their mechanical functions in a counterfeit of intelligence, slowing, degenerating imperceptibly until the last spark should go out.

Cudyk fingered the manuscript, which lay on the desk before him. It was the last thing he had written, and it would never be finished. He had hunted it up, this morning, out of nostalgia, or perhaps through some obscure working of that impulse that made him look out at the stars each night.

There were twenty pages, the first chapter of a book that was to have been his major work. It ended with the words:

"The only avenue of escape for humanity is..."

He had stopped there, because he had realized suddenly that he had been deliberately deceiving himself; that there was no avenue. The scheme he had meant to propose and develop in the rest of the book had one thing in common with those he had demolished in the first pages. It would not work.

Cudyk thought of those phantom chapters now, and was grateful that he had not written them. He had meant to propose that the exiles should band together on some un-peopled planet, and rear a new generation which would be given all the knowledge of the old, save for two categories: military science and astronomy. They would never be told, never guess that the bright lights of their sky were suns, that the suns had planets and the planets people. They would grow up free of that numbing pressure; they would have a fresh start.

It had been the grossest self-deception. You cannot put the human mind in chains. Every culture had tried it, and every culture had failed...

He pulled open a drawer of his desk and put the manuscript into it. A folded note dropped to the floor as he did so. Cudyk picked it up and read again:

You are requested to attend a meeting, which will be held at 8 Washington Avenue at 10 hours today. Matters of public policy will be discussed.

It was not signed; no signature was needed, nor any threatened alternative to complying with the "request". Cudyk glanced at his wristwatch, made on Oladi by spidery, many-limbed creatures to which an ordinary watch move-ment was a gross mechanism. The dial showed the Galactic Standard numerals, which corresponded, to ten o'clock.

Cudyk stood up wearily and walked out past the carved screen. He said to Nick, "I'll be back in an hour or so."

Eight Washington Avenue was The Little Bear, half a block from the corner where he had first met Harkway, a block and a half from the spot where Harkway's corpse had been left in a doorway. Two more associations, Cudyk thought. After twenty-five years, there were so many that he could not move a foot in the Quarter, glance at a window or a wall, without encountering one of them. And this was another thing to remember about a ghetto: you were crowded not only in space but also in time. The living were the most transient inhabitants of the Quarter.

Cudyk stepped through the open door of The Little Bear, saw the tables empty and the floor bare. The bartender, Piljurovich, jerked his thumb toward the stairs. "You're late," he said in Russian. "Better hurry."

Cudyk climbed the stairs to the huge second-floor-dining hall, where the Russians and Poles held their periodic revels. The room was packed tight with a silent mass of men. At the far end, Rack sat on a chair placed on a table. He stopped in mid-sentence, stared coldly at Cudyk, and then went on.

"—or against me. From now on, there won't be any more neutrals. I want you to understand this clearly. For one thing, your lives may depend on it."

He paused, glancing around the room. "By now you all know that James Harkway was executed last night. His crime was treason against the human race. There are some of you here who have been, or will be, guilty of the same crime. To them I have nothing more to say. To the others, those who have considered themselves neutral, I say this: First, New Earth needs all of you and has earned your allegiance. Second, those of you who remain on an enemy planet in spite of this warning will not live to regret it if that planet is selected for attack.

"You have two months to make up your minds and to close your affairs. At the end of that time, a New Earth transport will call here to take off those who decide to go. It will be the last New Earth ship, and I warn you that you had better not count on Galactic transportation after that date."

He stood up. "That's all."

The audience was over. Rack waited, standing on the

table, thumbs hooked into his belt, jacket over his shoulders, like a statue of himself, while the crowd moved slowly out of the room. It was ludicrous, but you could not laugh.

Two months. For almost twenty years Rack had been a minor disturbance in the Quarter, no more important or dangerous or mad than a dozen others; appearing suddenly, at night, staying for a few days, disappearing again for a month, or two, or six. He brought stolen goods to Ferguson—furs from Drux Uta, perhaps, or jewels from Thon—and Ferguson paid him in Galactic currency, reselling the merchandise later, some on Palumbar, some on a dozen other worlds, for twenty times the price he paid. Rack had a following among the younger men of the Quarter; two or three a year joined him. Occasionally there were rumors in the Quarter of Rack's close calls with the Galactic Guard. It had never been a secret that he was building military installations on some far-off planet. But now, for the first time, Cudyk realized that Rack was actually going to make war on the universe.

Whatever the result, the least it meant was the end of the Quarter.

The stairs were choked. Cudyk worked his way down, to find the barroom filled with little knots of men, talking in low voices. Only a few were drinking.

Someone called his name, and then a hand grasped his sleeve. It was Speros Moulios, the grey little tobacco dealer, whose two sons drank too much. "Mr. Cudyk, please, what do you think? Should we go, like he says?"

The others of the group followed him; in a moment Cudyk was surrounded. He felt helpless. "I can't advise you, Mr. Moulios," he said. "To be truthful, I don't know what I am going to do myself."

Nobilio Villaneuva, the druggist, said, "I have worked fifteen years, saved all my money. What am I going to do with it if I go to this New Earth? And what about my daughter?"

Someone came elbowing his way through the crowd. He signaled to Cudyk. "Laszlo!" It was bald, cheerful Mike Moskowitz, one of the Quarter's two doctors. He said, "Some of the fellows want to form a delegation, to go back and ask Rack some questions. They asked me to serve, but I've got to get back to the hospital. Same thing with Seu, he's got six things on his hands already. Father Exarkos isn't here. Will you take over? Good. I'll see you later."

Cudyk sighed. The men around him were watching him expectantly. He stepped over to the bar, picked up an empty glass and rapped with it on the counter until the room quieted.

"It's been suggested," he said, "that a delegation be formed to ask Captain Rack for more information. Do you all want that?"

There was an affirmative murmur.

"All right," said Cudyk. "Nominations?"

They ended up with a committee of five: Cudyk as spokesman, Moulios, Chong Yin, the painter Prokop Vekshin, and the town clerk, Martin Paz. Cudyk had slips of paper passed out, and collected a hundred-odd questions, most of them duplicates and some of them incoherent. Paz made a neat list of those that remained, and the delegation moved toward the stairs.

AT THE FOOT of the stairway Cudyk saw Burgess standing, blinking uncertainly around him. He dropped back and put his hand on the man's arm. "Hello, Louis. I'm glad to see you. How is Kathy?"

Burgess straightened a trifle. "Oh—Laszlo. She's all right, thank you. Feeling a little low, just now, of course..." His voice trailed off.

"Of course," said Cudyk sympathetically. "I wish there were something I could do."

"No—no, there's nothing. Time will cure her, I suppose. Where are you going now?"

Cudyk explained. "Were you at the meeting, earlier?" he asked.

"No. I was not invited. I only heard—ten minutes ago. Perhaps it would be all right if I came upstairs with you? In that way— But if I would be a nuisance—" His features worked.

Cudyk felt obscurely uneasy. He recalled suddenly that it was a long time since he had seen Burgess looking perfectly normal. He said reluctantly, "I think it will be all right. Why not? Come along."

Rack was sitting at the end of the long table on the far side of the room, talking to Ferguson. Ferguson's hatchet-man, Vic Smalley, was leaning watchfully against the far wall. Monk and Spider sat at Rack's left. De Grasse, pale and red-eyed, sat halfway down the table, away from the others. He stared at the table in front of him, paying no attention to the rest.

Cudyk had heard that De Grasse was still with Rack, and had wondered what he had done to expiate his sin. The obvious answer was one that he had not wanted to believe: that De Grasse had been given the task of murdering Harkway.

He had done it, probably, with a tormented soul and under Rack's eye, but he had done it. So much, Cudyk thought wearily, for the selfless nobility of man.

Rack looked up expressionlessly as the five men approached. "Yes?"

Cudyk said, "We have been chosen to ask you some questions about your previous statement."

"Ask away," said Rack, leaning back in his chair. Before

him was a glass of the dark, smoky liquor Ferguson imported for his special use. He was smoking a tremendously long, black Russian cigarette.

Cudyk took the list from Paz and read the first question. "What is the status of New Earth as to housing, utilities and so on?"

"Housing and utilities are adequate for the present population," said Rack indifferently. "More units will be built as needed."

Paz scribbled in his notebook. Cudyk read, "Will every new colonist be expected to serve as a member of New Earth's fighting forces?"

Rack said, "Every man will work where he's needed. Common sense ought to tell you that middle-aged men with pot bellies and no military training won't be asked to man battleships."

"What is the size of New Earth's navy?"

"Next question."

"Will new colonists be allowed to retain their personal fortunes?"

Rack stared at him coldly. "The man who asked that," He said, "had better stay in the Quarter. If by his personal fortune he means Galactic currency, he can use it to stuff rat-holes. Any personal property of value to the community, and in excess of the owner's minimum needs, will be commandeered and dispensed for the good of the community."

"Will new colonists be under military dis—"

"Look out!" said De Grasse suddenly. He lurched to his feet, upsetting his chair.

Someone stumbled against Paz, who fell heavily across Cudyk's legs, bringing him down. Someone else shouted. From the floor, Cudyk saw Burgess standing quietly with a tiny nickeled revolver in his hand.

"Please don't move, Mr. Ferguson," said Burgess. "I don't trust you. All of you stand still, please."

Cudyk carefully got his legs under him and slowly stood up. The men on the other side of the table were still sitting or standing where they had been a moment before. De Grasse stood in an attitude of frozen protest, one big hand flat against his trousers pocket. He looked comically like a man who has left the house without his keys.

They must have taken his gun away, Cudyk thought, after that affair yesterday.

Monk and the aged Spider were sitting tensely, trying to watch Rack and Burgess at the same time. Rack, as always, was inhumanly calm. Ferguson looked frightened. The gunman, Vic Smalley, had straightened away from the wall; he looked alert and unworried.

"Captain Rack," said Burgess, "you killed that man Harkway."

Rack said nothing.

"I did it," De Grasse said hoarsely. "If you have to shoot somebody, shoot me."

Burgess turned slightly. Rack, without seeming to hurry, picked up the glass in front of him and half rose to fling the black liquor at Burgess' face.

The gun went off. Burgess stumbled back a step and then toppled over, with a knife-handle sprouting magically between neck and shoulder. De Grasse came hurtling across the table top, dived onto Burgess' prostrate body and came up with the gun. Not more than two seconds had gone by since Rack lifted the glass.

The delegates were moving away, leaving a clear space around De Grasse and Burgess. Cudyk heard some of them clattering down the stairs.

Rack was leaning over the table, supporting himself with one hand, while the other rested at his waist. His attitude, together with his frozen expression, suggested that he was merely bending over to examine Burgess' body. But in the next moment he turned slightly, lifted the hand that was pressed to his side, and looked at the dark stain that was spreading over his shirt.

De Grasse stood up. Cudyk went to Burgess and knelt beside him. The man was conscious and moving feebly. "Lie still," said Cudyk. Someone pushed his shoulder roughly, and he looked up to see De Grasse transferring the revolver from his left hand to his right. The youngster's lips were compressed, "Get out of the way," he said harshly.

"No," said Rack. "Leave him alone." He sat down carefully. After a moment De Grasse went around the table and joined him.

Cudyk lifted Burgess' jacket carefully. There was not much bleeding, and he did not think the wound was dangerous. Burgess said weakly, "Did I kill him, Laszlo?"

"No," said Cudyk. "No one was killed."

Burgess turned his head away.

There were footsteps on the stairs, and Moskowitz came into the room, followed by Lee Far and two men with a stretcher. Moskowitz glanced at Burgess and at Rack, then knelt beside Burgess without a word. He pulled out the knife expertly, pressing a wad of bandage around the wound.

"I'll take that," said Spider, bending over with his grey hand outstretched.

Moskowitz dropped the knife on the floor and went on bandaging Burgess. Spider picked it up, glared at the doctor and went back around the table.

Cudyk waited until Moskowitz had finished with Burgess and started probing for the bullet in Rack's side. Following the stretcher-bearers down the stairs, he went out into the clear morning sunlight.

CHAPTER FIVE

There was never any end to it. The Quarter was like a tight gravitational system, with many small bodies swinging around each other in eccentric orbits, and the whole shrinking in upon itself as time went on, so that it grew more and more certain that one collision would engender half a dozen more.

And in the mind, too, each event went on forever. Cudyk remembered Burgess, in the stretcher as he was being carried home, weeping silently because he had failed to kill the man who had murdered his daughter's lover. And he remembered Rack, sitting silent and weary as he waited for Moskowitz to attend to him: sitting without anger for the man who had shot him, sitting with patience, filled with his own inner strength.

And De Grasse, tortured soul, who had once more shown himself willing to sacrifice himself to any loyalty he felt.

Even Monk, even Spider, lived not for himself but for Rack.

There were all the traditional virtues, dripping their traditional gore: nobility, self-sacrifice, patience, even generosity. By any test except the test of results, Rack was a great man and Burgess another.

And the test of results was a two-edged razor: for by that test, Cudyk himself was a total failure, a nonentity.

He thought, *We are the hollow men, we are the stuffed men...*

When every action led to disaster, those who did nothing were damned equally with those who acted.

SOMEONE touched Cudyk's arm as he left Chong Yin's. He turned and saw that it was Ferguson.

"I've got something to say to you, Cudyk. I saw you were busy talking to Father Exarkos in there, so I didn't bother you. Besides, it's private. Come on down to my place."

The man was doing him an honor, Cudyk realized, in approaching him personally instead of sending an underling. And now, as Ferguson stood waiting for him to reply, Cudyk saw that there was something curiously like appeal in his eyes.

"All right, if you wish," he said. "But I will have to go back to the shop within an hour—Nick has not had his lunch."

"I won't keep you that long," Ferguson said.

They turned at the corner and walked down Washington, past Town Hall to The Little Bear. Beyond this point, everything was Ferguson's: the dance hall, the casino, the bawdy house, the two cafes and three bars, and the two huge warehouses at the end of the avenue. But it was the casino that Ferguson meant when he said "my place".

A white-aproned boy got up hurriedly and opened the heavy doors when they approached. Ferguson strode past without looking at him, and Cudyk followed across the long, empty room. Dust covers shrouded the roulette table, the chuck-a-luck layout, faro, chemin-de-fer, dice and poker tables. The bar was deserted, bottles and glasses neatly stacked.

Ferguson led the way up a short flight of stairs to the overhanging balcony at the end of the room. He opened the door with a key—a rarity in the Quarter, since cylinder locks were available only by scavenging on Earth, and had to be imported, whereas a mechanism used by the Niori as a mathematical toy could be readily adapted into an efficient combination lock.

The low-ceilinged room was furnished with a blond-wood desk and swivel chair, a long, pale green couch and two chairs upholstered in the same fabric: all Earth imports, scavenged from stocks manufactured before the Collapse. The carpet was a deeper green. There were three framed pictures on the walls: a blue-period Picasso, a muted oyster white and grey Utril-lo and a small Roualt clown.

Ferguson was watching him. "Just like my place in Chicago," he said. "You never saw it before, did you?"

"No," Cudyk said. "I have never been in the Casino until now."

"Sit down," said Ferguson, pointing to one of the upholstered chairs. He pulled out the swivel chair and leaned back in it. He nodded toward the glass, which formed the entire front wall of the room. "Sittin' up here, I can see everything that goes on downstairs. I got a phone—" he laid his hand on it—"that communicates with the cashier's booth in every room. I can handle the whole place from here, and I don't have to be bothered by the goofs if I don't want to. Also, that glass is bullet proof. It's Niori stuff, ten times better than anything we had back home. They tell me you couldn't get through it with a bazooka."

Cudyk said nothing.

"What I wanted to talk to you about—" said Ferguson, leaning forward with his elbows on his knees. "You understand, Cudyk, this is confidential. Strictly between us."

"I don't want any confidence that will be difficult to keep," said Cudyk.

"What do you mean?"

"If it is something that touches the safety of the Quarter—"

Ferguson waved his hand impatiently. "No, it's nothing like that. I just don't want it to get around too early. All right, use your own judgment. Here it is."

"Rack's coming back in about three weeks with his transport, to pick up anybody that wants to go to New Earth. I'm not going, and neither are any of my boys. On the other hand, I'm not going to stay here either. It isn't healthy any more."

"I don't know what Rack's got, but I've got a pretty good idea he's got enough to raise a lot of hell. Now you can figure the angles for yourself: maybe he won't bomb this planet because he thinks he can still make some use of the Quarter—but that's a big maybe. Even if he doesn't, it's a dead cinch there's going to be trouble. The Niori know he comes here, even if they can't prove it, and when the war starts they're going to be sore."

"Tell me something," said Cudyk after a moment. "If you knew all this long ago—and you must have, since you have been so closely associated with Rack—why did you help Rack, and so force yourself to leave Palumbar?"

Ferguson grinned and shrugged, "I'm not complaining," he said. "Rack never fooled me. I got mine, and he got his— it was a business arrangement. When you figure everything in, I can clear out now and I'm still ahead. See, you got to figure that nothing lasts forever. If I hadn't played along with Rack, he would have taken his business somewhere else. Maybe I could have stayed here a little longer, but then again, maybe I would have stayed too long. This way, I got my information in advance, and I got my profit from dealing with Rack.

"As a matter of fact, he thinks me and all my outfit are going to be on that transport when it goes back to his base. He knows I wouldn't take a chance on staying here when the shooting starts. What he doesn't know is that I got someplace else to go, and a way to get there."

He sat back in his chair again. "I got a Niori-built freighter hidden back in the hills. Had it for eight years now. It'll carry five hundred people, and fuel and provisions for a year, on top of the cargo. And I got a planet picked out where nobody will bother me—not Rack, and not the Galactics."

He took a cigar box from the desk and offered it to Cudyk. Cudyk shook his head, showing his pipe.

Ferguson took a cigar, twirled it in his lips slowly, and lit it. "You know," he said, bending forward, "there's plenty of planets in the galaxy that aren't inhabited. Some have never even been explored. They're off the shipping routes, no intelligent race on them, nothing special in the way of organic products, so nobody wants them. Rack's got one—I've got another."

He gestured with the cigar. "But I'm not using mine to build up any war base. What for?" His long face contorted with violent disgust. "That Rack is crazy. You know it and I know it. If it wasn't for him, I could have stayed here, who knows how long? Or I could have moved to one of the other colonies if I saw a good chance. I like it here. This is civilization—all that's left of it.

"But—" he leaned back again—"you got to take what you can get. If the odds are too heavy, cash in and walk out. That's what I'm doing: I'm retiring. On this planet I told you about, there's a big island. A tropical island. Fruit—all you can eat. Little animals something like wild pigs. Fish in the ocean. Gravity just a little under Earth normal, atmosphere perfect. And I'm taking along everything else we'll need. Generators, all kinds of electrical equipment, stoves, everything. It'll last your lifetime and mine."

He looked at Cudyk. "What more would you want?"

Cudyk said slowly, "You're asking me to go with you?"

Ferguson nodded. "Sure. I'll treat you right, Cudyk. My boys will go on working for me, you understand, and so will most of the others I'm going to take. I'll be the boss. But you, and three or four others, you won't have to do any work. Just lie in that sand, or go fishing, or whatever you feel like. How does it sound?"

"I don't think I quite understand," said Cudyk. "Why do

46

you choose me?"

Ferguson put down his cigar. He looked uncomfortable. He said irritably, "Because I've got to have somebody to talk to." He stared at Cudyk. "Look at me. Here I am, I'm fifty years old, and I been fighting the world ever since I was a kid. You think I can just cut loose from everything now, and lie under a tree? I'd go nuts in a month. I'm not kidding myself, I know what I am. It takes practice to learn how to relax and enjoy yourself. I never learned, never had the time.

"When I get on that island, and I get all the houses built and the wires strung up, and everything's organized and I've got nothing else to do, I can see myself lying there thinking about this place, and all the other places I ever owned, and thinking to myself, 'What for?' And there's no answer, I know that. But just the same, I'm going to be wanting to start in again, making a deal, opening a joint, figuring the angles, handling people.

"So there I'll be, with all these mugs around me. What do they know to talk about? The same things I do. Things that happened to them in the rackets, here or back on Earth. You got to talk to somebody, or you go crazy. But if I've got nobody but them to talk to, how'm I ever going to get my mind off that kind of stuff?"

He gestured toward the Roualt, on the wall to Cudyk's left. "Look at that," he said. "I bought that thing in 1991. I've been looking at it for; let's see, twenty-three years. For the first five or so I couldn't figure out whether the guy was kidding or not. Then, gradually, I got to like it. But I still don't know *why* the hell I like it. It's the same thing with everything. I have a Corot that I'm nuts about—I look at it every night before I go to sleep. It's just a landscape, like you used to see on calendars in the old days, except the calendars were junk and this is art. I know that, I can feel it. But what's the difference between the two? Don't ask me.

"See what I mean? That's the kind of stuff I got to learn about. Art. Literature. Music. Philosophy. I always wanted to, before, but I never had the patience for it. Now I've *got* to do it. My kind of life is finished; I've got to learn a new kind."

He frowned at his cigar. "It isn't going to be easy. Maybe there'll be times when you'll wish you had anybody else in the world around but me. But I won't take it out on you, Cudyk."

He meant it, Cudyk knew. For a moment he wondered, why don't I accept? He could see Ferguson's island paradise clearly enough: the tropical trees, the log huts—with electric light, induction stoves for cooking, and hot and cold water—the sand, the sunshine, the long, lazy afternoons spent in talking quietly on the beach. There would be no strain and no tension, if everything went as Ferguson planned—only a long, slow twilight, with nothing left to fear or to hope for: forgetfulness, lethargy; lotos and Lethe; a pleasant exile, a scented prison.

"You won't have to worry about the others, the guys that work for me," Ferguson said. "After they get through building the settlement, they can do what they want as long as they don't make any trouble. There'll be enough women to go around—they can settle down and raise kids. There won't be any liquor, and I'm going to keep the weapons locked up. About the ship—I'll wreck that as soon as we land. Once we're there, we're there."

If it were not for Ferguson himself, Cudyk thought, I believe I might do it. But Ferguson, inside a year, is going to be a pitiable and terrible object. This is his own punishment, his lesser evil—he chooses it himself. But he is not going to like it.

"I think I understand," he said. "Believe me, Mr. Ferguson, I'm deeply grateful for this offer, and I am tempted to accept. But—I think I will stay and take my chances with the Quarter."

Ferguson stared at him, and then shrugged. "Don't make up your mind in too much of a hurry," he said. "Think it over—I'm not leaving for a couple of weeks. And listen, Cudyk, do me a favor. Don't spread this around."

"Very well," said Cudyk.

Ferguson did not get up to see him to the door.

CHAPTER SIX

THERE WAS a curious feeling of suspension in the Quarter. Trade was slow; only a few Niori and still fewer members of other Galactic races strolled down the narrow streets, and for more than a week Cudyk sold nothing.

Human faces were missing, too. Almost two hundred of the ghetto's inhabitants had left quietly, during the night, when word had gone around that the "New Earth" transport was waiting. Villanueva had gone, with his family; so had Martin Paz; and Ferguson had gone earlier with all his crew. Today, two weeks later, Cudyk had spent the morning wandering the City. It was a thing he had done often in his first years on the planet, before the restless drive of his youth had seeped away, leaving nothing but momentum, and memory, and a few vestiges that reminded him of the man he had been.

He had spent whole days in the City, then, looking into this building and that, talking to the natives, asking questions, observing. He had seen the City as part of a colossal jigsaw puzzle from which, if you were patient and perceptive, you might extract the nexus, the inner pattern that made the essential difference between Niori and men.

For the Niori, like nearly all the intelligent races of the galaxy, had one survival factor that men had always lacked.

There was no word for it in any human language; you could only talk around it in negatives. The Niori did not kill; they did not lie; they did not steal, intrigue, exploit each other, hate, or make war.

For men, "the fittest" had always been the man, or nation, or race that survived by exterminating its rivals. Somehow, the Niori had found another way. There was no word for it. But perhaps you could find it, if you looked long enough.

He had studied their architecture, and pondered long on the arrangement of the City's great hive-buildings: a peculiar, staggered arrangement which was neither concentric nor radial; which created no endless vistas, only islands of buildings or lakes of parkland. He had tried to see into that arrangement and through it to the soul of the race, as other scholars had peered into the city-plans of Athens and New York, reading inwardness into one and outwardness into the other.

The method was sterile. The Niori had no "world-view" in the Spenglerian sense. Their cities expressed only function and a sense of beauty and order.

In those early days, he had said to himself: These people have no cinemas, theaters, churches, art galleries, concert halls, football fields. Let me see what they have instead, and perhaps I will begin to understand them.

He had seen the Niori, sitting in a circle of six or eight, solemnly capping one word with another, around and around. To him, the sequences of words were sense-free and followed no discern able pattern. To the Niori, evidently, they fulfilled some function analogous to those of poetry and group singing.

He had watched them debating in the governing council. There was no rhetoric and no heat, even when the issue was important and the opinions widely divergent. He had seen their shops, in which each article was labeled with its cost to the merchant, and the buyer gave as much more as he could afford. It was incredible; but it worked.

He had followed their culture through a thousand other avenues until he wearied of it, having learned nothing more than he knew at the beginning. Afterwards, for twenty years he had not left the Quarter except to transact business, or to oversee the unloading of merchandise at the spaceport.

Today he had gone once more, feeling an obscure compulsion: perhaps because he knew the day was coming when he would see the City for the last time; perhaps hoping, in that small spark of himself that still allowed itself to hope for anything, that one more visit would show him the miraculous key to all that he had misunderstood.

He had learned nothing new, but the morning had not been altogether wasted. It was a clear autumn day, good for walking in so green a city. And paradoxically enough, being the only Earthman on the streets had made him feel less alien than before. He attracted no attention, in a spaceport city: he walked side by side with squat Dritik and spidery Oladsa, beings of a hundred different races from as many stars. When he returned to the Quarter, he felt oddly refreshed and calmed.

We have very little left, he thought, except one or two minor virtues that have no bloodstains on them. Kindliness, humor, a sense of brotherhood...perhaps if we had stuck to those, and never learned the martial virtues, never aspired to be noble or glorious, we would have come out all right. Was there ever a turning point? When Carthage was sown with salt, or when Paul founded the Church—or when the first caveman sharpened the end of a stick and used it for murder? If so, it was a long way back, dead and buried, dust and ashes.

We took all that was best in thousands of years of yearning and striving for the right, he thought, and we made it into the Inquisition and the Star Chamber and the NKVD. We fattened our own children for each generation's slaughter. And yet we are not all evil. Astereos is right: if the other races had been like ourselves, it would have been bearable; or if we ourselves had been creatures of pure darkness, conscienceless, glorying in cruelty—then we could have made war on the Galaxy joyfully, and if we failed at least there would have been an element of grandeur in our failure.

Olaf Stapledon had said this once, he remembered—that there was artistry in pure, uncontaminated evil, that it was in its own way as real an expression of worship as pure good.

The tragedy of human beings, then, was that they were not wholly tragic. Jumbled, piebald parcels of contradictions, angels with asses' ears... What was that quotation from Bierce? *The best thing is not to be born...*

Someone brushed by him, and Cudyk looked up. He was at the intersection of Ceskoslovensko and Washington; he had come three blocks past his apartment without noticing where he was going.

Chong Yin's was only a few doors to his left; perhaps he had been heading there automatically. But the doors were closed, he saw; seven or eight Chinese were standing in the street outside, and as Cudyk watched, Seu Min came down the stairs from the living quarters over the tea room. The other Chinese clustered around him for a moment, and then Seu appeared again. The others slowly began to disperse.

Cudyk went to meet him. The mayor's face looked strained; there were new, deep folds of skin around his eyes. "What is it, Min?" said Cudyk.

Seu fell in beside him and they walked back up the street. "Chong killed himself about an hour ago," said the Chinese.

How many does that make? Cudyk thought, frozen. Six, I think, in the last two months.

He had not known Chong well—the old man had been a north-country Chinese, not Westernized in the least, who spoke only his own language. Now that he thought of it, Cudyk realized that he did not know who Chong's close friends had been, if he had had any. He had always been the same spare, stooped figure in skullcap and robe, courteous, unobtrusive, and self-contained. He had a family; a wife, rarely seen, and six children.

Somehow Cudyk felt that he would have been less surprised to hear that Moulios had committed suicide, or Moskowitz, or even Seu himself. My mistake, he told himself. I allowed myself to think of Chong as an institution, not as a man.

"Have you some whiskey?" asked Seu abruptly.

"Yes," said Cudyk, "of course."

"Let us go and drink it," Seu said. "I'm very tired."

It occurred to Cudyk that he had never heard Seu say that before. They turned the corner at Athenai and climbed the stairs to his apartment. Seu sighed, and dropped heavily into a chair while Cudyk went to get the bottle and glasses.

"Straight, or with water?" he asked.

"Straight, please." Seu tilted his glass, swallowed and shuddered. Cudyk watched him in silence.

Seu, alone in the Quarter, owned a Niori communicator— an elaborate mechanism that reproduced sound, vision in three dimensions, odors, modulated temperature changes and several other things perceptible only to Niori. There was no restriction on their sale, and they were cheap enough, but the Niori broadcasts were as dull or as incomprehensible to men as a Terrestrial breakfast program would have been to Niori. Seu used his as a source of Galactic news. Today, Cudyk guessed, the news had been very bad.

"It's Rack, isn't it?" he said finally.

Seu glanced at him and nodded. "Yes, it's Rack. I haven't told anyone else about it yet. The Quarter's in a half-hysterical state as it is. But if you don't mind my talking it out to you—"

"Go ahead," said Cudyk.

"It's worse than anything we expected." Seu took another swallow of the whisky, and made a face. He said, "They've got a hydrogen-lithium bomb."

"…I was afraid of that."

Seu went on as if he had not heard. "But they're not using it on planets. They're bombing suns, Laszlo."

For a moment, Cudyk did not understand, then he felt his abdominal muscles contract like a fist. "They couldn't," he said hoarsely. "It would explode before it got past the outer layers."

"Under faster-than-light drive?" Seu asked. "I did some figuring. At 1000 C, it would take the bomb about two point six thousandths of a second to travel from the surface to the center of an average G-class star. I think that is a short enough interval, but maybe it isn't. Maybe they have also found some way to increase the efficiency of the standard galactic drive for short periods. Anyway, does it matter?" He looked at Cudyk again. "I have seen the pictures. I *saw* it happen."

Cudyk's throat was dry. "Which stars?" he said.

"Törkas. Rud-Uri. That's the Oladi sun. And Gerzión. Those three, so far."

Cudyk's fingers were nervously caressing the smooth metal of his wristwatch. He looked down at it suddenly, remembering that the Oladsa had made it. And now they were gone, all but their colonies and travelers on other worlds, and those who had been in space at the time. All those spidery, meticulous people, with their million-year-old culture and their cities of carved opal, wiped out as a man would swat a fly.

Seu took another drink. His face flushed, and drops of sweat stood out on his forehead and cheeks.

He said, "They'll have to learn to kill, now. There isn't any alternative. They intercepted one of the New Earth ships and sprayed it with the stasis field. It didn't work; the ship got away. They'll have to learn to kill. Do you know what that means?"

"Yes."

Seu drank again. His face was fiery red, now, and he was gasping for breath. "I can't get drunk," he said bitterly. "Toxic reaction. I thought I'd try once more, but it's no good. Laszlo, look out, I'm going to be sick."

Cudyk led him to the lavatory. When he came out, the Chinese was weak and waxen-pale. Cudyk tried to persuade him to rest on the bed, but he refused. "I've got to get back to my office," he said. "Been gone too long already. Help me down the stairs, will you, Laszlo?"

Cudyk walked him as far as Brasil and Washington, where two of Seu's young men took over with voluble expressions of gratitude. Cudyk watched the group until it disappeared into the town hall.

He could feel nothing but an arid depression. Even the horror at Rack's mass-murders, even his pity for Seu was blunted, sealed off at the back of his mind. The lives of saints, Cudyk remembered, spoke of "boundless compassion", "infinite pity"; but an ordinary man had a limited supply. When it was used up, you were empty and impotent, a canceled sign in the human equation.

Half instinctively, half by choice, Cudyk had chosen his friends among the strongest and most patient, the wise and cynical: the survivors. But he had leaned too much on their strength, he realized now. He had seen Seu crumble; and he felt as if a crutch had broken under his weight.

That evening he opened his shutters and looked out at the sky. The familiar constellations were there, unchanged. The light of the nearest star took more than three years to reach

Palumbar. But in his mind's eye one glittering pinpoint exploded suddenly into a dreadful blossom of radiance; then another; then a third. And he saw the blackened corpses of planets swinging around each, murdered by that single flash of incredible heat.

During the night he dreamed of a black wasteland, and of Rack standing motionless in the center of it, brooding, with his cold grey face turned to the stars.

CHAPTER SEVEN

IT WAS Cudyk's birthday. He had never told anyone in the Quarter the date, and had all but forgotten it himself. This morning, feeling an idle desire to know what the season was on Earth, he had hunted up a calendar he had last used twenty years ago; it translated the Niori system into Gregorian years, months and days. The result, when he had worked it out with some little trouble, was February 18th. He was fifty-six.

Now he was constrained to wonder whether the action had been as random as it seemed. Was it possible that subconsciously he had no need of the calendar—that he had kept track, all these years, and had known when his birthday came? If so, why had he felt it necessary to remind himself in this oblique way?

A return to the womb? A hunger for the comforts of the family circle, the birthday cake, candles, the solace of yearly repetition?

Cudyk was fifty-six. When he had been fifty-five, he had thought of himself as a man in his middle years, still strong, still able. Now he was old. The same thing had happened to Seu: he had recovered from his first shock when the news had come about Rack, and for more than three weeks now he had moved about the Quarter, as quiet and as competent as before; but there was a difference. His swift, furtive humor was gone except for rare flashes; his voice and his step were heavy.

It was the same with all of them, all the old settlers. Cudyk had met Burgess on the street the day before, for the first time in several weeks, and had been genuinely shocked. The man's hair was white, his skin papery, his gait stumbling.

Even Exarkos showed the change. More and more of his grey, woolly hair was vanishing. The umber crescents under his eyes were a deeper shade, almost black.

The Quarter's graveyard was five acres of ground, surrounded by trees, on the outskirts of the City; there the dead reclined in a more ample space than the living enjoyed. The Niori had allotted the ground, though the outline of the City was thereby disfigured, and had contributed slabs of a synthetic stone, which carved easily when it was fresh, later hardening until it would resist any edged tool. The plot was ill tended, but the standing stones, translucent pearl or rose, had a certain beauty. To the Niori, the purpose of the graveyard was only that; they were not equipped to understand mankind's morbid clinging to its own carrion.

Cudyk had gone to Chong's funeral, presided over by Lee Yuk, the asthmatic little Buddhist priest; and the image of those ranked headstones, neatly separated into the Orthodox, the Protestants, the Buddhists, the Taoists and the un-believers, had returned to him many times since. It was another sign of the change that was taking place in him: the images which formerly had dominated his mind had been pictographs of abstractions—the great globe of infinity, the tiny spark that was creative intellect. Now they were the pale headstone and the dark curtain of death.

He had felt nothing, standing over Chong's grave and watching the sod fall. What is there to say about a man when he is dead? The priest's words were false, as all such words are false; they had no relevance; the man was dead. Nothing was left of him now but the dissolving molecules of his flesh, and the fragmentary, ego-distorted memories he had planted in the minds of others. He was a name written in water.

It was not Chong who obsessed Cudyk, nor the many other half-remembered men and women whose names were clumsily carved on those stones. It was the cemetery as a symbol: the fascination of the yawning void.

Cudyk had one other preoccupation: he thought often of Earth, a dark globe turning, black continents dim against the grey ocean, pricked by a few faint gleams that were cities. Or, if he thought of the cities, he saw them too drowned in shadow: the shapes of tower and arch melting into night-patterns; moonlight falling faintly, dissolving what it touched, so that shadows became as solid stone, stone as insubstantial mist.

For Earth, also, was a symbol of death.

There had been no more suicides since Chong had died, and no riots. It seemed to Cudyk that the whole Quarter moved, like himself, through a fluid heavier than air. All motion had slowed, and sounds came muted and without resonance. People spoke to him, and he answered, but without attention, as if they were not really there.

Even the recent news about Rack's defeat had stirred him only momentarily, and he had seen in Seu's face that the Chinese felt himself somehow inadequate to the tale even as he told it. The Galactic fleet, vastly expanded, had met Rack's activist forces with a new weapon—one, indeed, which did not kill, but which was shameful enough to a citizen of the Galaxy. The weapon projected a field, which scrambled the synapse patterns in the brain, leaving its victim incapable of any of the processes of coherent thought: incapable of adding two figures, of lighting a cigarette, or of aiming a torpedo. Eleven New Earth ships had been captured, and it was thought that these were all the activists' armed vessels; there had been no further attacks since then.

He did not believe that anything, which could now possibly happen, could rouse him from his apathy. But he had forgotten one possibility. Seu came to him in Chong Yin's, where Yin's eldest son Fu now moved in his father's place, and said, "Rack wasn't taken. He's here."

Cudyk sat with his teacup raised halfway between the table and his lips. After a long moment, he saw that his hand was trembling violently. He set the cup down. He said. "Where?"

"The Little Bear. Half the town has gone there already. Do you want to go?"

Cudyk stood up slowly. "Yes," he said, "I suppose so." But he felt the tension that pulled his body together, he tautened muscles in back and shoulders and arms.

As they reached the corner of Ceskoslovensko and Washington, they saw scattered groups of men moving ahead of them, all hurrying, some frankly running. The crowd was thick around the doorway of The Little Bear when they reached it, and they had difficulty forcing a passage. Men moved aside for Seu willingly enough, but there was little space to move.

Inside, it was worse. The stairway was solidly packed; it was obviously impossible to get through.

"There is a back stair," Seu said. He worked his way toward the rear of the room, Cudyk following, until he caught sight of the bartender. The press was not so thick here, and he was able to reach the man and lead him into a corner away from the others. "Can you get us up the back way?"

The Russian nodded, scowled, and put his finger to his lips. Following him, they went through the swinging doors at the back of the room, through the dark kitchen and up the narrow service stairs at the rear. The bartender unlocked the door and helped them force it open against the pressure of the packed bodies inside.

The long room was heavy with the odors of sweat, tobacco smoke and stale air. Faces shone greasily under the glare of the ceiling lights. The only clear space was the table-top against the wall to Cudyk's right, where Rack stood.

Cudyk could see him clearly over the heads of those in front of him. He stood with legs planted firmly, hands at his sides. As always, the leather jacket was draped over his shoulders like a cloak.

He was alone. Spider was not there, nor Monk, nor Tom De Grasse.

Rack was talking in a low, clear voice. Cudyk listened to the end of a sentence, which conveyed nothing to him, and then heard: "After that, we got it. They gave it to us." Rack's hands clenched once, and then opened again.

"They intercepted us three minutes after we came out of overdrive in the orbit of New Earth. Twelve fighting ships, the whole fleet. We were in a line, just closing in after we broke C on the way down—the *Thermopolae*, the *Tours*, the *Waterloo*, the *Chateau Thierry*, the *Dunkirk*, the *Leningrad*, the *Acre*, the *Valley Forge*, the *Hiroshima*, the *San Francisco*, the *Seoul*, and the flagship last, the *Armageddon*.

"We didn't know they were there—they were out of our detector range. They had us like sitting ducks. The first thing we knew about it was when a teletype report from the leading ship, the *Thermopolae*, broke off in the middle of a word. Five seconds later the same thing happened to a report coming in from the next ship. Three seconds more, and the *Waterloo* was gone.

"I gave the order to reverse acceleration and scatter. But the field—whatever it was—came after us. It would have taken us at least two minutes to build up the overdrive potential again, and we all knew we wouldn't make it. They were getting us one ship every six or eight seconds.

"The men were looking to me for orders. I didn't have any to give them. Suddenly De Grasse turned around and looked at Monk and Spider, and they all nodded. They jumped me. I don't know what happened. I struck my head against the deck when I went down, or one of them hit me with a gun-butt."

His fists clenched and opened once more. "When I came to, I was strapped into a one-man lifeboat, on overdrive, doing ten C's. They must have emptied the ship's accumulators into that lifeboat, charged it up to C potential and got me off just before the field hit them.

"I took my bearings, reversed, and went back. Eventually I found the fleet again. The Galactics had matched course and velocity with them and they were just beginning to tow them off, one ship to one with plenty of theirs left over, in the general direction of Altair.

"They hadn't got into overdrive yet. I slipped in—there were a hundred of their little scouts nosing around, about the same mass as my lifeboat—and berthed in the same port I'd come out of. I got out and walked into the control room.

"The crew was still there, still alive. But not men. They were lying on the deck, looking at nothing. Their mouths were open, and they were drooling."

Rack's head moved stiffly, and his sharp profile turned from one side of the crowd to the other. "Mindless idiots," he said. "They couldn't feed themselves, or stand up, or sit. But they had saved me.

"I built up the charge and took my time about it. When the Galactics went into overdrive, I took off in another direction. I was a good seventy light years away before they knew I was gone.

"I had a ship, an undamaged ship. But I had no crew to

man her. I can astrogate, and when I have to, I can man the engines on top of that. But I can't fight her as well.

"I came here, put the *Armageddon* into a one-day orbit and came down in a lifeboat. I want to go back and find out what those slime-eaters did to us, and give them a taste of the same. *I want twenty men.*"

There was a silence.

Rack said, in the same even, low voice, "Will you fight for the human race?"

Someone called, "What did you do with your other crew?"

Rack said, "I gave them military burial, in space."

For the first time, the crowd as a whole broke its silence. A low murmur rose. Rack said sharply, "I would have given my life for those men, as they did for me, gladly. But they were already dead. If there's a way to restore a man's mind after that has been done to it, only the vermin know how. I would rather be buried in space, and so would they."

A deep voice called, "Are you God, Rack?"

"I'm not God," he said promptly. "Are you a man?"

There was another murmur, dying as a pulsing movement began near the back of the room: someone was forcing his way toward Rack. In the stillness, another voice said thinly, "My Demetrios…my Alexander…" It was Moulios, wailing for his two lost sons.

Red-faced, with a lock of hair hanging over his forehead, the painter Vekshin squeezed through to the edge of the table on which Rack stood. He shouted, "I'm a man, all right. What do you call yourself, you assassin? You come here with blood dripping from your jaws like a weasel fresh from a poultry yard, and we're supposed to feel sorry because they wouldn't let you go on killing! The great god Rack! *Ptui!*"

Rack did not move. He said quietly, "I killed your enemies, while you sat at home and drank tea."

"Enemies!" Vekshin roared. "You're the enemy, Rack." He put his big hands on the tabletop and heaved himself up.

Rack let him come. He waited until the Russian was standing on the table; then he stepped forward with a motion so smooth it seemed casual. There was a flurry of blows, none of which landed except two: one in Vekshin's midriff, the other on the point of his jaw. Five men went down as Vekshin's body hurtled into them.

Rack stepped back. "I have very little patience left," he said, "but if there is anyone else here with a personal grudge, let him step up."

Two men at the table's edge moved as if to climb up. Rack put his hand to the gun at his belt. The two men stayed where they were.

Rack stared out over the crowd.

He looked suddenly very weary. It occurred to Cudyk that he must have gone without sleep for a long time.

Rack said: "This is the last call. I am not trying to deceive you. I promise you nothing, not glory, not your lives, not even that you will be able to spend your lives usefully. But if there is any man here who will serve aboard the *Armageddon*, in the last fight for mankind—raise your hand!"

There was a long moment's silence. Rack turned abruptly, with his hand still on his gun, and said to the men in front of Cudyk: "Stand back!"

The silence held for an instant, while the men at the table's end moved uncertainly away; then sound broke like an avalanche. As Rack jumped down, the crowd surged toward him, no longer an audience but a mob. Cudyk felt the pressure at his back, caught a glimpse of Rack's face, and then heard the deafening report of the gun as he went hurtling forward into the melee.

The gun did not fire again. Cudyk was squeezed tightly in the center of the struggling mass. He saw Seu, a few feet away. The mayor's mouth was open; he was shouting something, but the words were lost.

Suddenly Rack came into view again, charging straight toward Cudyk, hurling bodies to either side. The lower half of his face was a smear of blood; his cap and jacket were gone, his shirt torn half away.

Cudyk was half-aware of the constriction in his throat, the pounding of blood at his temples. He wrenched one arm free and, as Rack came near, struck him full in the face.

He had one more glimpse of Rack's white features, the pale eyes staring at him with a curiously detached expression: the eyes of a Caesar or a Christ, reproachful and sad. Then the crowd surged once more, the door to the back stairway slammed open, and Rack was gone.

Cudyk found himself running through the doorway with half a dozen others. He caught sight of Rack leaping down the stairs, just short of the landing where the narrow stairway doubled back on itself.

With a regretful sigh, feeling no surprise at what he was about to do, Cudyk put both hands on the railing and swung himself over into vacancy. Then there was an instant of wild, soaring flight, Rack's foreshortened body drifting beneath him, and the shock.

Dazed and numb, Cudyk felt the universe moving under him like a gigantic pendulum. He saw faces appear and vanish, felt someone push him aside, heard voices faintly.

After a long time his head cleared, and there was silence. He was lying at the foot of the stairs, one arm flung over the first step. Rack was not there; no one was there but himself.

He moved cautiously and was rewarded by an astonishing number and variety of pains. But apparently he had broken no bones. He felt weak and hollow; he was afraid he might vomit. He hoisted his torso up slowly, sat on the lowest step and then put his head between his trembling knees.

He heard a foot scuff on the concrete floor, and looked up. It was Seu.

The Chinese looked at him anxiously. "You're all right?"

"Yes. I think so. I have felt better in my life."

"Do you want to get up? Did you jump or fall?"

Cudyk leaned forward, trying the strength of his thighs to raise him, and Seu put a hand under his arm to help. "I jumped," Cudyk said. "What happened, afterward?"

"The mob came down, me in the middle, and I couldn't stop to see if you were all right. They took Rack with them. He was unconscious then; he may have been dead."

"And?"

"They tore him apart," said Seu.

They moved toward the exit from the kitchen, Seu holding Cudyk's arm firmly.

"I don't know if you felt this," the mayor said stiffly, "but the way it seemed to me was that Rack suddenly represented all of it—not only the bombings, but the Quarter, the Galaxy, Earth—everything we hated. It was a feeling of release, a kind of ecstasy. Watch out for the sill."

"Scapegoat," Cudyk said, indistinctly.

"Yes...Zydh Oran saw it, you know. He was there when the mob came out. He saw it all. This finishes the Quarter, Laszlo. After this there won't be any more reprieves."

Cudyk glanced down at Seu's plump fingers. There was a thin film of blood on the skin, and a dark line of it around each fingernail.

CHAPTER EIGHT

CUDYK stood at the top of the gentle rise opposite the Washington Avenue Bridge, and looked down at the Quarter. It was just after sunset, and the ranked streetlights cast a lonesome gleam. The streets were empty. There was no one left in the Quarter except one man in the powerhouse. When the time was up, he would pull the switches on the master board and come out; then the Quarter would be dead.

The Niori edict had come on the Wednesday morning after Rack's death. They had been given four days to pack their belongings, arrange for assignment of cargo space, and wind up their several affairs. Cudyk's stock was small and his personal belongings few; he had been ready two days ago.

The evening breeze, freshening, pressed Cudyk's trousers against his calves and stirred the hair at the back of his head. Looking into the east, he saw a few pallid stars in the sky.

Several hundred people had already been collected by the aircars, which served the spaceport. Cudyk, Seu, Exarkos and a few others, by unspoken assent, had taken places at the rear of the crowd, to be the last to go.

He glanced at Seu. The little man was standing with his hands in his pockets; shoulders slumped, staring dully at the Quarter. He looked up after a moment, smiled unhappily, and shrugged.

"It's absurd to feel homesick for it, isn't it?" he said. "It was a ghetto; we had no roots there. It was cramped, and it stank, and we fought among ourselves more viciously than we ever fought on Earth. But twenty years…"

"We could pretend that we had roots, at least," Cudyk answered. "We don't belong anywhere. Perhaps we'll be happier, in the long run, once we face that and accept it."

"I doubt it."

"So do I."

To Cudyk's right, Father Exarkos was sitting on his suitcase, hands relaxed on his thighs. Cudyk said, "If I were a believer, Astereos, I think it would do me a great deal of good to confess to you and be absolved."

The priest's dry, friendly voice said, "Why, have you

sinned so terribly, Laszlo?"

"I killed a man," said Cudyk, "but that's not what I mean. I jumped over a stairway railing and stopped Rack. If it hadn't been for me, he might have got away. There would have been nothing wrong with that. He couldn't have done any more harm, one man by himself. The Guards would have captured him sooner or later, anyhow. And if he had gotten away, we wouldn't have given the Niori the one more straw they needed. In that sense, it is my fault that we were expelled."

"No, Laszlo," said Seu.

Exarkos said, "You have nothing for which to reproach yourself, on that score. You were only the instrument of history, my friend, and a minor instrument at that. And, speaking for myself, not for the Church, Rack deserved to die."

Cudyk thought, at least it was quite suitably ironic. Cudyk, the man of inaction, hurls himself through the air to kill a murderer. And the citizens of the Quarter are deported, not because one of their race murdered a billion billion Galactics, but because that same killer was killed by them.

That was one thin mark on the credit side. There was one more: the tension was gone, for some of them at least. Now the worst thing that could happen had happened; the Damocletian thread had snapped. The problems, which had caused the tension no longer existed.

Earth was two months away. Cudyk expected nothing and hoped for nothing. But the Niori had agreed to set each passenger down wherever on the globe he chose to go; each man, at least, could choose his own hell. The crews of the captured battleships, and the captured staff of the base on New Earth, were also being sent back. The weapon that had been used on them had done no permanent damage; they would simply have to be retrained, to learn all over again, as if they were reborn.

Seu was going to North America, where he hoped survival for a fat cosmopolite would be a little less difficult than in Europe or Asia. Moskowitz had been born in New York, and was going back there. Exarkos was going to Istanbul first, for orders; he had no idea where he might be sent after that. Cudyk had not yet made up his mind. He thought that perhaps he would go with the priest; if he should change his mind after landing it would be no great loss; one wilderness, as Exarkos had once said, was as good as another.

It will all be anticlimax, he thought, and perhaps that is the definition of Hell: unending anticlimax.

He wondered how it would feel to be Earthbound again. The repatriation ship was to be the last Galactic vessel, which would ever call at Earth. And there would be a constant guard. The Niori had learned, belatedly but well. If humanity ever climbed high enough again to reach the stars with its bloody fingers, the citizens of the galaxy would be ready.

Cudyk looked at his watch. The man in the powerhouse must be a sentimentalist; he was waiting until the last possible moment.

He heard the soft hum of the aircar behind him, turned and saw it settling lightly to the clipped lawn. The remaining passengers were moving toward it. Exarkos stood up and lifted his suitcase. Cudyk turned back for one last look at the Quarter. It was full dark now, and all he could see of it was the blocky, ambiguous outline of its darkness against the glowing buildings beyond, and the crosshatched pattern of yellow streetlights.

The lights went out.

THE END

COSMOS CONFIDENTIAL

The authorized history of the frontier worlds of the 29th century is readily available to anyone who cares to pore through the official files of the Terrestrial Diplomatic Corps.

For serious students of history, however, it would be well to read between the lines of what has been set down by posterity. The records, for example, fail to grasp the full significance of the work done by a career diplomat named James Retief, in his efforts to alleviate strife on the emerging planets of our galaxy.

Contained here are several accounts of Retief's contributions to the peace of the universe—written in the hope that the injustices committed by the history books will thus be rectified.

TABLE OF CONTENTS

ENVOY TO NEW WORLDS

By KEITH LAUMER

ARMCHAIR FICTION
PO Box 4369, Medford, Oregon 97504

For more information about Armchair Books and products, visit our website at…

www.armchairfiction.com

Or email us at…

armchairfiction@yahoo.com

"...into the chaotic Galactic political scene of the post-Concordiat era, the CDT emerged to carry forward the ancient diplomatic tradition as a great supranational organization dedicated to the contravention of war. As mediators of disputes among Terrestrial-settled worlds and advocates of Terrestrial interests in contacts with alien cultures, Corps diplomats, trained in the chanceries of innumerable defunct bureaucracies, displayed an encyclopedic grasp of the nuances of Estra-Terrestrial mores as set against the labyrinthine socio-politico-economic Galactic context. Never was the virtuosity of a senior Corps diplomat more brilliantly displayed than in Ambassador Spradley's negotiation of the awkward Sirenian Question..."

—extract from the *Official History of the Corps Diplomatique,* Vol I, reel 2. Solarian Press, New New York, 479 A. E. (AD 2940)

PROTOCOL

IN THE GLOOM of the squat, mud-colored reception building, the Counselor, two First Secretaries, and the senior Attaches gathered around the plump figure of Ambassador Spradley, their ornate diplomatic uniforms bright in the vast gloomy room. The Ambassador glanced at his finger watch impatiently.

"Ben, are you quite certain our arrival time was made clear?"

Second Secretary Magnan nodded emphatically. "I stressed the point, Mr. Ambassador. I communicated with Mr. T'Cai-Cai just before the lighter broke orbit, and I specifically emphasized—"

"I hope you didn't appear truculent, Mr. Magnan," the Ambassador cut in sharply.

"No indeed, Mr. Ambassador. I merely—"

"You're sure there's no VIP room here?" The Ambassador glanced around the cavernous room. "Curious that not even chairs have been provided."

"If you'd care to sit on one of those crates, I'll use my hanky—"

"Certainly not." The Ambassador looked at his watch again and cleared his throat.

"I may as well make use of these few moments to outline our approach for the more junior members of the staff. It's vital that the entire mission work in harmony in the presentation of the image. We Terrestrials are a kindly, peace-loving race." The Ambassador smiled in a kindly, peace-loving way.

"We seek only reasonable division of spheres of influence with the Yill." He spread his hands, looking reasonable.

"We are a people of high culture, ethical, sincere."

The smile was replaced abruptly by pursed lips. "We'll start by asking for the entire Sirenian System, and settle for half. We'll establish a foothold on all the choicer worlds and, with shrewd handling, in a decade we'll be in a position to assert a wider claim." The Ambassador glanced around. "If there are no questions…"

Jame Retief, Vice-Consul and Third Secretary in the Corps Diplomatique and junior member of the Terrestrial Embassy to Yill, stepped forward.

"Since we hold the prior claim to the system, why don't we put all our cards on the table to start with? Perhaps if we dealt frankly with the Yill, it would pay us in the long run."

Ambassador Spradley blinked up at the younger man. Beside him, Magnan cleared his throat in the silence.

"Vice-Consul Retief merely means—"

"I'm capable of interpreting Mr. Retief's remark," Spradley snapped. He assumed a fatherly expression.

"Young man, you're new to the service. You haven't yet learned the team play, the give-and-take of diplomacy. I shall expect you to observe closely the work of the experienced negotiators of the mission, learn the importance of subtlety. Excessive reliance on direct methods might tend in time to attenuate the role of the professional diplomat. I shudder to contemplate the consequences."

Spradley turned back to his senior staff members. Retief strolled across to a glass-paneled door and glanced into the room beyond. Several dozen tall gray-skinned Yill lounged in deep couches, sipping red drinks from slender glass tubes. Black-tuniced servants moved about discreetly, offering trays. Retief watched as a party of brightly-dressed Yill moved toward an entrance door. One of the party, a tall male, made to step before another, who raised a hand languidly, fist clenched. The first Yill stepped back and placed his hands on top of his head with a nod. Both Yill continued to smile and chatter as they passed through the door.

Retief rejoined the Terrestrial delegation, grouped around a mound of rough crates stacked on the bare concrete floor, as a small leather-skinned Yill came up.

"I am P'Toi. Come thiss way..." He motioned. The Terrestrials moved off, Ambassador Spradley in the lead. As the portly diplomat reached the door, the Yill guide darted ahead, shouldering him aside, then hesitated, waiting. The Ambassador almost glared, then remembered the image. He smiled, beckoning the Yill ahead. The Yill muttered in the native language, stared about, then passed through the door. The Terran party followed.

"I'd like to know what that fellow was saying," Magnan said, overtaking the Ambassador. "The way he jostled your Excellency was disgraceful."

A number of Yill waited on the pavement outside the building. As Spradley approached the luxurious open car waiting at the curb, they closed ranks, blocking his way. He drew himself up, opened his mouth—then closed it with a snap.

"The very idea," Magnan said, trotting at Spradley's heels as he stalked back to rejoin the staff, now looking around uncertainly. "One would think these persons weren't aware of the courtesies due a Chief of Mission."

"They're not aware of the courtesies due an apprentice sloat skinner!" Spradley snapped. Around the Terrestrials, the Yill milled nervously, muttering in the native tongue.

"Where has our confounded interpreter betaken himself?" The Ambassador barked. "I daresay they're plotting openly..."

"A pity we have to rely on a native interpreter."

"Had I known we'd meet this rather uncouth reception," the Ambassador said stiffly, "I would have audited the language personally, of course, during the voyage out."

"Oh, no criticism intended, of course, Mr. Ambassador," Magnan said hastily. "Heavens, who would have thought—" Retief stepped up beside the Ambassador.

"Mr. Ambassador," he said, "I—"

"Later, young man," the Ambassador snapped. He beckoned to the Counselor, and the two moved off, heads together.

A bluish sun gleamed in a dark sky. Retief watched his breath form a frosty cloud in the chill air. A broad hard-wheeled vehicle pulled up to the platform. The Yill gestured the Terran party to the gaping door at the rear, then stood back, waiting.

Retief looked curiously at the grey-painted van. The legend written on its side in alien symbols seemed to read 'eggnog'. Unfortunately he hadn't had time to learn the script too, on the trip out. Perhaps later he would have a chance to tell the Ambassador he could interpret for the mission.

The Ambassador entered the vehicle, the other Terrestrials following. It was as bare of seats as the Terminal building. What appeared to be a defunct electronic chassis lay in the center of the floor, amid a litter of paper and a purple and yellow sock designed for a broad Yill foot. Retief glanced back. The Yill were talking excitedly. None of them entered the car. The door was closed, and the Terrans braced themselves under the low roof as the engine started up with a whine of worn turbos, and the van moved off.

It was an uncomfortable ride. The unsprung wheels hammered uneven cobblestones. Retief put out an arm as the vehicle rounded a corner, caught the Ambassador as he staggered off-balance. The Ambassador glared at him, settled his heavy tri-corner hat, and stood stiffly until the car lurched again.

Retief stooped, trying to see out through the single dusty window. They seemed to be in a wide street lined with low buildings. They passed through a massive gate, up a ramp, and stopped. The door opened. Retief looked out at a blank grey facade, broken by tiny windows at irregular intervals. A scarlet vehicle was drawn up ahead, the Yill reception committee emerging from it. Through its wide windows Retief saw rich upholstery and caught a glimpse of glasses clamped to a tiny bar.

P'Toi, the Yill interpreter, came forward, gesturing to a small door in the grey wall. Magnan scurried ahead to open it and held it for the Ambassador. As he stepped to it a Yill thrust himself ahead and hesitated. Ambassador Spradley drew himself up, glaring. Then he twisted his mouth into a frozen smile and stepped aside. The Yill looked at each other, then filed through the door.

Retief was the last to enter. As he stepped inside a black-clad servant slipped past him, pulled the lid from a large box by the door and dropped in a paper tray heaped with refuse.

There were alien symbols in flaking paint on the box. They seemed, Retief noticed, to spell 'eggnog'.

The shrill pipes and whining reeds had been warming up for an hour when Retief emerged from his cubicle and descended the stairs to the banquet hall. Standing by the open doors he lit a slender cigar and watched through narrowed eyes as obsequious servants in black flitted along the low wide corridor, carrying laden trays into the broad room, arranging settings on a great four-sided table forming a hollow square that almost filled the room. Rich brocades were spread across the center of the side nearest the door, flanked by heavily decorated white cloths. Beyond, plain white extended down the two sides to the far board, where metal dishes were arranged on the bare tabletop. A richly dressed Yill approached, stepped aside to allow a servant to pass and entered the room.

Retief turned at the sound of Terran voices behind him. The Ambassador came up, trailed by two diplomats. He glanced at Retief, adjusted his ruff and looked into the banquet hall.

"Apparently we're to be kept waiting again," he snapped. "After having been informed at the outset that the Yill have no intention of yielding an inch, one almost wonders…"

"Mr. Ambassador," Retief said, "Have you noticed—"

"However," Ambassador Spradley said, eyeing Retief, "A seasoned diplomatist must take these little snubs in stride. In the end—ah there, Magnan…" He turned away, talking.

Somewhere a gong clanged. In a moment the corridor was filled with chattering Yill who moved past the group of Terrestrials into the banquet hall. P'Toi, the Yill interpreter, came up, raised a hand.

"Waitt heere…"

More Yill filed into the dining room, taking their places. A pair of helmeted guards approached and waved the Terrestrials back. An immense grey-jowled Yill waddled to the doors, ropes of jewels clashing softly, and passed through, followed by more guards.

"The Chief of State," Retief heard Magnan say. "The Admirable F'Kau-Kau-Kau."

"I have yet to present my credentials," Ambassador Spradley said. "One expects some latitude in the observances of protocol, but I confess…" He wagged his head.

The Yill interpreter spoke up.

"You now whill lhie on yourr intesstinss and creep to fesstive board there." He pointed across the room.

"Intestines?" Ambassador Spradley looked about wildly.

"Mr. P'Toi means our stomachs, I wouldn't wonder," Magnan said. "He just wants us to lie down and crawl to our seats, Mr. Ambassador."

"What the devil are you grinning at, you idiot?" the Ambassador snapped.

Magnan's face fell.

Spradley glanced down at the medals across his paunch.

"This is… I've never…"

"Homage to godss," the interpreter said.

"Oh-oh—religion," someone said.

"Well, if it's a matter of religious beliefs…" The Ambassador looked around dubiously.

"Actually, it's only a couple of hundred feet," Magnan said.

Retief stepped up to P'Toi.

"His Excellency, the Terrestrial Ambassador will not crawl," he said clearly.

"Here, young man, I said nothing—"

"Not to crawl?" The interpreter wore an unreadable Yill expression.

"It is against our religion," Retief said.

"Againsst?"

"We are votaries of the Snake Goddess," Retief said. "It is a sacrilege to crawl." He brushed past the interpreter and marched toward the distant table. The others followed.

Puffing, the Ambassador came to Retief's side as they approached the dozen empty stools on the far side of the square opposite the brocaded position of the Admirable F'Kau-Kau-Kau.

"Mr. Retief, kindly see me after this affair," he hissed. "In the meantime, I hope you will restrain any further rash impulses. Let me remind you *I* am Chief of Mission here."

Magnan came up from behind.

"Let me add my congratulations, Retief," he said. "That was fast thinking."

"Are you out of your mind, Magnan?" the Ambassador barked. "I am extremely displeased."

"Why," Magnan stuttered, "I was speaking sarcastically, of course, Mr. Ambassador. Naturally I, too, was taken aback by his presumption."

The Terrestrials took their places, Retief at the end. The table before them was of bare green wood, with an array of shallow pewter dishes upon it.

The Yill at the table, some in plain grey, others in black, eyed them silently. There was a constant stir among them as one or another rose and disappeared and others sat down. The pipes and reeds of the orchestra were shrilling furiously and the susurration of Yillian conversation from the other tables rose ever higher in competition. A tall Yill in black was at the Ambassador's side now. The nearby Yill all fell silent as the servant ladled a whitish soup into the largest of the bowls before the Terrestrial envoy. The interpreter hovered, watching.

"That's quite enough," Ambassador Spradley said, as the bowl overflowed. The Yill servant dribbled more of the soup into the bowl. It welled out across the tabletop.

"Kindly serve the other members of my staff," the Ambassador commanded. The interpreter said something in a low voice. The servant moved hesitantly to the next stool and ladled more soup.

Retief watched, listening to the whispers around him. The Yill at the table were craning now to watch. The servant was ladling the soup rapidly, rolling his eyes sideways. He came to Retief and reached out with the full ladle for the bowl.

"No," Retief said.

The servant hesitated.

"None for me," Retief said.

The interpreter came up, motioned to the servant, who reached again, ladle brimming.

"I don't want any!" Retief said, his voice distinct in the sudden hush. He stared at the interpreter, who stared back for a moment, then waved the servant away and moved on.

"Mr. Retief," a voice hissed. Retief looked down the table. The Ambassador was leaning forward, glaring at him, his face a mottled crimson.

"I'm warning you, Mr. Retief," he said hoarsely. "I've eaten sheep's eyes in the Sudan, *ka swe* in Burma, hundred-year cug on Mars, and everything else that has been placed before me in the course of my diplomatic career, and by the holy relics of Saint Ignatz, you'll do the same!" He snatched up a spoon-like utensil and dipped it into his bowl.

"Don't eat that, Mr. Ambassador," Retief said.

The Ambassador stared, eyes wide. He opened his mouth, guiding the spoon toward it.

Retief stood, gripped the table under its edge, and heaved. The immense wooden slab rose and tilted; dishes crashed to the floor. The table followed with a ponderous slam. Milky soup splattered across the terrazzo; a couple of odd bowls rolled clattering across the room. Cries rang out from the Yill, mingling with a strangled yell from Ambassador Spradley.

Retief walked past the wild-eyed members of the mission to the sputtering chief. "Mr. Ambassador," he said. "I'd like—"

"You'd like! I'll break you, you young hoodlum! Do you realize—"

"Pleass…" The interpreter stood at Retief's side.

"My apologies," Ambassador Spradley said, mopping his forehead. "My profound—"

"Be quiet," Retief said.

"Wh-what?!"

"Don't apologize," Retief said.

P'Toi was beckoning. "Pleasse, arll come."

Retief turned and followed him.

The portion of the table they were ushered to was covered with an embroidered white cloth, set with thin porcelain dishes. The Yill already seated there rose, amid babbling and moved down to make room for the Terrestrials. The black-clad Yill at the end table closed ranks to fill the vacant seats. Retief sat down, finding Magnan at his side.

"What's going on here?" the Second Secretary said.

"They were giving us dog food," Retief said. "I overheard a Yill. They seated us at the servants' section of the table."

"You mean you understand the language?"

"I learned it on the way out—enough, at least—"

The music burst out with a shrill fanfare, and a throng of jugglers, dancers, and acrobats poured into the center of the hollow square, frantically juggling, dancing, and back-flipping. Servants swarmed, heaping mounds of fragrant food on the plates of Yill and Terrestrials alike, pouring pale purple liquor into slender glasses. Retief sampled the Yill food. It was delicious. Conversation was impossible in the din. He watched the gaudy display and ate heartily.

Retief leaned back, grateful for the lull in the music. The last of the dishes were whisked away, and more glasses filled. The exhausted entertainers stopped to pick up the thick square coins the diners threw. Retief sighed. It had been a rare feast.

"Retief," Magnan said in the comparative quiet. "What were you saying about dog food as the music came up?"

Retief looked at him. "Haven't you noticed the pattern, Mr. Magnan? The series of deliberate affronts?"

"Deliberate affronts! Just a minute, Retief. They're uncouth, yes, crowding into doorways and that sort of thing. But..." He looked at Retief uncertainly.

"They herded us into a baggage warehouse at the terminal. Then they hauled us here in a garbage truck."

"Garbage truck!"

"Only symbolic, of course. They ushered us in the tradesmen's entrance, and assigned us cubicles in the servants' wing. Then we were seated with the coolie-class sweepers at the bottom of the table."

"You must be mistaken! I mean, after all, we're the Terrestrial delegation; surely these Yill must realize our power."

"Precisely, Mr. Magnan. But—"

With a clang of cymbals, the musicians launched a renewed assault. Six tall, helmeted Yill sprang into the center of the floor paired off in a wild performance, half dance, half combat. Magnan pulled at Retief's sleeve, his mouth moving. Retief shook his head. No one could talk against a Yill orchestra in full cry. Retief sampled a bright red wine and watched the show.

There was a flurry of action, and two of the dancers stumbled and collapsed, their partner-opponents whirling away to pair off again, describe the elaborate pre-combat ritual, and abruptly set to, dulled sabers clashing—and two more Yill were down, stunned. It was a violent dance. Retief watched, the drink forgotten.

The last two Yill approached and retreated, whirled, bobbed, and spun, feinted and postured. And then one was slipping, going down, helmet awry, and the other, a giant, muscular Yill, spun away, whirled in a mad swirl of pipes as coins showered—then froze before a gaudy table, raised the sabre, and slammed it down in a resounding blow across the gay cloth before a lace-and-bow-bedecked Yill. The music stopped with a ringing clash of cymbals.

In utter silence the dancer-fighter stared across the table. With a shout the seated Yill leaped up and raised a clenched fist. The dancer bowed his head, spread his hands on his helmet and resumed his dance as the music blared anew. The beribboned Yill waved a hand negligently, flung a handful of coins across the floor, and sat down.

Now the dancer stood rigid before the brocaded table— and the music chopped off short, as the saber slammed down before a heavy Yill in ornate metallic coils. The challenged Yill rose, raised a fist, and the other ducked his head, putting his hands on his helmet. Coins rolled, and the dancer moved on.

He circled the broad floor, saber twirling, arms darting in an intricate symbolism. Then suddenly he was towering before Retief, saber above his head. The music cut, and in the startling instantaneous silence, the heavy saber whipped over and down with an explosive concussion that set dishes dancing on the tabletop.

The Yill's eyes held on Retief's. In the silence Magnan tittered drunkenly. Retief pushed back his stool.

"Steady, my boy," Ambassador Spradley called. Retief stood, the Yill topping his six-foot-three by an inch. In a motion too quick to follow Retief reached for the saber, twitched it from the Yill's grasp, swung it in a whistling arc. The Yill ducked, sprang back and snatched up a saber dropped by another dancer.

"Someone stop the madman!" Spradley howled.

Retief leaped across the table, sending fragile dishes spinning.

The other danced back, and only then did the orchestra spring to life with a screech and a mad tattoo of high-pitched drums.

Making no attempt to follow the weaving pattern of the Yill bolero, Retief pressed the Yill, fending off vicious cuts with the blunt weapon, chopping back relentlessly. Left hand on hip, Retief matched blow for blow, driving the other back.

Abruptly the Yill abandoned the double role. Dancing forgotten, he settled down in earnest, cutting, thrusting, parrying. Now the two stood toe to toe, sabers clashing in a lightning exchange. The Yill gave a step, two, then rallied, drove Retief back, back—

Retief feinted, laid a hearty whack across the grey skull. The Yill stumbled, his saber clattered to the floor. Retief stepped aside as the Yill wavered past him and crashed to the floor.

The orchestra fell silent in a descending wail of reeds. Retief drew a deep breath and wiped his forehead.

"Come back here, you young fool!" Spradley called hoarsely.

Retief hefted the saber, turned, and eyed the brocade-draped table. He started across the floor. The Yill sat as if paralyzed.

"Retief, no!" Spradley yelped.

Retief walked directly to the Admirable F'Kau-Kau-Kau, stopped, raised the saber.

"Not the Chief of State," someone in the Terrestrial Mission groaned.

Retief whipped the saber down. The dull blade split the heavy brocade and cleaved the hardwood table. There was utter silence.

The Admirable F'Kau-Kau-Kau rose, seven feet of obese grey Yill. His broad face expressionless to the Terran eye, he raised a fist like a jewel-studded ham.

Retief stood rigid for a long moment. Then, gracefully, he inclined his head and placed his fingertips on his temples. Behind him there was a clatter as Ambassador Spradley collapsed. Then the Admirable F'Kau-Kau-Kau cried out, reached across the table to embrace the Terrestrial, and the orchestra went mad. Grey hands helped Retief across the table, stools were pushed aside to make room at F'Kau-KauKau's side. Retief sat, took a tall flagon of coal-black brandy pressed on him by his neighbor, clashed glasses with The Admirable, and drank.

"The feast ends," F'Kau-Kau-Kau said. "Now you and I, Retief, must straddle the Council Stool."

"I'll be honored, Your Admirableness," Retief said. "I must inform my colleagues."

"Colleagues?" F'Kau-Kau-Kau said. "It is for chiefs to parley. Who shall speak for a king while he yet has tongue for talk?"

"The Yill way is wise," Retief said.

F'Kau-Kau-Kau emptied a squat tumbler of pink beer. "I'll treat with you, Retief, as viceroy, since as you say your king is old and the space between worlds is far. But there shall be no scheming underlings privy to our dealings." He grinned a Yill grin. "Afterwards we shall carouse, Retief. The Council Stool is hard, and the waiting handmaidens delectable; this makes for quick agreement."

Retief smiled. "The Admirable speaks wisdom."

"Of course, a being prefers wenches of his own kind," F'Kau-Kan-Kau said. He belched. "The Ministry of Culture has imported several Terrestrial joy-girls, said to be topnotch specimens. As least they have very fat watchamacallits."

"Your Admirableness is most considerate," Retief said.

"Let us to it then, Retief. I may hazard a tumble with one of your Terries, myself. I fancy an occasional perversion." F'Kau-Kau-Kau dug an elbow into Retief's side and bellowed with laughter.

As Retief crossed to the door at F'Kau-Kau-Kau's side, Ambassador Spradley glowered from behind the plain tablecloth. "Retief," he called, "kindly excuse yourself. I wish a word with you." His voice was icy. Magnan stood behind him, goggling.

"Forgive my apparent rudeness, Mr. Ambassador," said Retief. "I don't have time to explain now—"

"Rudeness!" Spradley yipped. "Don't have time, eh? Let me tell you—"

"Please lower your voice, Mr. Ambassador," Retief said. "The situation is still delicate."

Spradley quivered, his mouth open. He found his voice, "You! —you—"

"Silence!" Retief snapped. Spradley looked up at Retief's face, staring for a moment into Retief's grey eyes. He closed his mouth and swallowed.

"The Yill seem to have gotten the impression I'm in charge," Retief said. "We'll have to maintain the deception."

"But—but—" Spradley stuttered. Then he straightened. "That is the last straw," he whispered hoarsely. "*I* am the Terrestrial Ambassador Extraordinary and Minister Plenipotentiary. Magnan has told me that we've been studiedly and repeatedly insulted, since the moment of our arrival; kept waiting in baggage rooms, transported in refuse lorries, herded about with servants, offered swill at the table.

Now I, and my senior staff, are left cooling our heels, without so much as an audience, while this—this multiple Kau person hobnobs with—with—"

Spradley's voice broke. "I may have been a trifle hasty, Retief, in attempting to restrain you. Slighting the native gods and dumping the banquet table are rather extreme measures, but your resentment was perhaps partially justified. I am prepared to be lenient with you." He fixed a choleric eye on Retief.

"I am walking out of this meeting, Mr. Retief. I'll take no more of these personal—"

"That's enough," Retief said sharply. "We're keeping The Admirable waiting."

Spradley's face purpled.

Magnan found his voice. "What are you going to do, Retief?"

"I'm going to handle the negotiation," Retief said. He handed Magnan his empty glass. "Now go sit down and work on the Image."

At his desk in the VIP suite aboard the orbiting Corps vessel, Ambassador Spradley pursed his lips and looked severely at Vice-Consul Retief.

"Further," he said, "you have displayed a complete lack of understanding of Corps discipline, the respect due a senior officer, even the basic courtesies. Your aggravated displays of temper, ill-timed outbursts of violence, and almost incredible arrogance in the assumption of authority make your further retention as an Officer-Agent of the Corps Diplomatique Terrestrienne impossible. It will therefore be my unhappy duty to recommend your immediate—"

There was a muted buzz from the communicator. The Ambassador cleared his throat.

"Well?"

"A signal from Sector HQ, Mr. Ambassador," a voice said.

"Well, read it," Spradley snapped. "Skip the preliminaries…"

"Congratulations on the unprecedented success of your mission. The articles of agreement transmitted by you embody a most favorable resolution of the difficult Sirenian situation, and will form the basis of continued amicable relations between the Terrestrial States and the Yill Empire. To you and your staff, full credit is due for a job well done. Signed, Deputy Assistant Secretary Sternwheeler."

Spradley cut off the voice impatiently. He shuffled papers, then eyed Retief sharply.

"Superficially, of course, an uninitiated observer might leap to the conclusion that the ah…results that were produced in spite of these…ah…irregularities justify the latter." The Ambassador smiled a sad, wise smile. "This is far from the case," he said. "I—"

The communicator burped softly.

"Confound it." Spradley muttered.

"Yes?"

"Mr. T'Cai-Cai has arrived," the voice said. "Shall I—"

"Send him in, at once." Spradley glanced at Retief. "Only a two-syllable man, but I shall attempt to correct these false impressions, make some amends…"

The two Terrestrials waited silently until the Yill Protocol chief tapped at the door.

"I hope," the Ambassador said, "that you will resist the impulse to take advantage of your unusual position." He looked at the door. "Come in."

T'Cai-Cai stepped into the room, glanced at Spradley, then turned to greet Retief in voluble Yill. He rounded the desk to the Ambassador's chair, motioned him from it, and sat down.

"I have a surprise for you, Retief," he said in Terran. "I myself eave made use of the teaching machine you so kindly lent us.

"That's good," Retief said. "I'm sure Mr. Spradley will be interested in hearing what we have to say."

"Never mind," the Yill said. "I am here only socially." He looked around the room.

"So plainly you decorate your chamber; but it has a certain austere charm." He laughed a Yill laugh.

"Oh, you are a strange breed, you Terrestrials. You surprised us all. You know, one hears such outlandish stories. I tell you in confidence. We had expected you to be overpushes."

"Pushovers," Spradley said tonelessly.

"Such restraint! What pleasure you gave to those of us, like myself of course, who appreciated your grasp of protocol. Such finesse! How subtly you appeared to ignore each overture, while neatly avoiding actual contamination. I can tell you, there were those who thought—poor fools—that you had no grasp of etiquette. How gratified we were, we professionals, who could appreciate your virtuosity—when you placed matters on a comfortable basis by spurning the cats-meat. It was sheer pleasure then, waiting, to see what form your compliment would take."

The Yill offered orange cigars, then stuffed one in his nostril.

"I confess even I had not hoped that you would honor our Admirable so signally. Oh, it is a pleasure to deal with fellow professionals, who understand the meaning of protocol."

Ambassador Spradley made a choking sound.

"This fellow has caught a chill," T'Cai-Cai said. He eyed Spradley dubiously. "Step back, my man, I am highly susceptible.

"There is one bit of business I shall take pleasure in attending to, my dear Retief," T'Cai-Cai went on. He drew a large paper from his reticule. "His Admirableness is determined that none other than yourself shall be accredited here. I have here my government's exequatur confirming you as Terrestrial Consul-General to Yill. We shall look forward to your prompt return."

Retief looked at Spradley.

"I'm sure the Corps will agree," he said.

"Then I shall be going," T'Cai-Cai said. He stood up. "Hurry back to us, Retief. There is much that I would show you of the great Empire of Yill." He winked a Yill wink.

"Together, Retief, we shall see many high and splendid things."

* * * *

...In the face of the multitudinous threats to the peace arising naturally from the complex Galactic situation, the polished techniques devised by Corps theoreticians proved their worth in a thousand difficult confrontations. Even anonymous junior officers, armed with briefcases containing detailed instructions, were able to soothe troubled waters with the skill of experienced negotiators. A case in point was Consul Passwyn's incisive handling of the Jaq-Terrestrial contretemps at Adobe...

Vol. II, reel 91 480 A. E. (AD 2941)

SEALED ORDERS

"IT'S TRUE," Consul Passwyn said, "I requested assignment as Principle Officer at a small post. But I had in mind one of those charming resort worlds, with only an occasional visa problem, or perhaps a distressed spaceman or two a year. Instead, I'm zoo-keeper to these confounded settlers, and not for one world, mind you, but eight." He stared glumly at Vice-Consul Retief.

"Still," Retief said, "it gives an opportunity for travel."

"Travel!" the Consul barked. "I hate travel. Here in this backwater system particularly..." He paused, blinked at Retief, and cleared his throat. "Not that a bit of travel isn't an excellent thing for a junior officer. Marvelous experience."

He turned to the wall-screen and pressed a button. A system triagram appeared: eight luminous green dots arranged around a larger disc representing the primary. Passwyn picked up a pointer, indicating the innermost planet.

"The situation on Adobe is nearing crisis. The confounded settlers—a mere handful of them—have managed, as usual, to stir up trouble with an intelligent indigenous life form, the Jaq. I can't think why they bother, merely for a few oases among the endless deserts. However, I have, at last, received authorization from Sector Headquarters to take certain action."

He swung back to face Retief. "I'm sending you in to handle the situation, Retief—under sealed orders." He picked up a fat, buff envelope. "A pity they didn't see fit to order the Terrestrial settlers out weeks ago, as I suggested. Now it's too late. I'm expected to produce a miracle—a rapprochement between Terrestrial and Jaq and a division of territory. It's idiotic. However, failure would look very bad in my record, so I shall expect results." He passed the buff envelope across to Retief.

"I understood that Adobe was uninhabited," Retief said, "until the Terrestrial settlers arrived."

"Apparently that was an erroneous impression. The Jaq are there." Passwyn fixed Retief with a watery eye. "You'll follow your instructions to the letter. In a delicate situation such as this, there must be no impulsive, impromptu element introduced. This approach has been worked out in detail at Sector; you need merely implement it. Is that entirely clear?"

"Has anyone at Headquarters ever visited Adobe?"

"Of course not. They all hate travel too. If there are no other questions, you'd best be on your way. The mail run departs the dome in less than an hour."

"What's this native life form like?" Retief asked, getting to his feet.

"When you get back," said Passwyn, "you tell me."

The mail pilot, a leathery veteran with quarter-inch whiskers, spat toward a stained corner of the compartment, and leaned close to the screen.

"They's shootin' goin' on down there," he said. "Them white puffs over the edge of the desert."

"I'm supposed to be preventing the war," said Retief. "It looks like I'm a little late."

The pilot's head snapped around. "War," he yelped. "Nobody told me they was a war goin' on on 'Dobe. If that's what that is, I'm gettin' out of here."

"Hold on," said Retief. "I've got to get down. They won't shoot at you."

"They shore won't, sonny. I ain't givin' 'em the chance." He reached for the console and started punching keys. Retief reached out, catching his wrist.

"Maybe you didn't hear me. I said I've got to get down."

The pilot plunged against the restraint and swung a punch that Retief blocked casually. "Are you nuts?" the pilot screeched. "They's plenty shootin' goin' fer me to see it fifty miles out."

"The mails must go through, you know."

"I ain't no consarned postman. If you're so dead set on gettin' killed—take the skiff. I'll tell 'em to pick up the remains next trip—if the shootin's over."

"You're a pal. I'll take your offer."

The pilot jumped to the lifeboat hatch and cycled it open. "Get in. We're closin' fast. Them birds might take it into their heads to lob one this way."

Retief crawled into the narrow cockpit of the skiff. The pilot ducked out of sight, came back, and handed Retief a heavy old-fashioned power pistol. "Long as you're goin' in, might as well take this."

"Thanks." Retief shoved the pistol in his belt. "I hope you're wrong."

"I'll see they pick you up when the shootin's over—one way or another."

The hatch clanked shut; a moment later there was a jar as the skiff dropped away, followed by heavy buffeting in the backwash from the departing mail boat. Retief watched the tiny screen, his hands on the manual controls. He was dropping rapidly: forty miles, thirty-nine...

At five miles, Retief threw the light skiff into maximum deceleration. Crushed back in the padded seat, he watched the screen and corrected the course minutely. The planetary surface was rushing up with frightening speed. Retief shook his head and kicked in the emergency retro-drive. Points of light arced up from the planet face below. If they were ordinary chemical warheads the skiff's meteor screens should handle them. The screen on the instrument panel flashed brilliant white, then went dark. The skiff leaped and flipped on its back; smoke filling the tiny compartment. There was a series of shocks, a final bone-shaking concussion, then stillness, broken by the ping of hot metal contracting.

Coughing, Retief disengaged himself from the shockwebbing, groped underfoot for the hatch, and wrenched it open. A wave of hot jungle air struck him. He lowered himself to a bed of shattered foliage, got to his feet...and dropped flat as a bullet whined past his ear.

He lay listening. Stealthy movements were audible from the left. He inched his way forward and made the shelter of a broad-baled dwarf tree. Somewhere a song lizard burbled. Whining insects circled, scented alien life, and buzzed off. There was another rustle of foliage from the underbrush five yards away. A bush quivered, then a low bough dipped. Retief edged back around the trunk and eased down behind a fallen log. A stocky man in a grimy leather shirt and shorts appeared, moving cautiously, a pistol in his hand.

As he passed, Retief rose, leaped the log, and tackled him. They went down together. The man gave one short yell, then struggled in silence. Retief flipped him onto his back, raised a fist—

"Hey!" the settler yelled. "You're as human as I am!"

"Maybe I'll look better after a shave," said Retief. "What's the idea of shooting at me?"

"Lemme up—my name's Potter. Sorry 'bout that. I figured it was a Flap-jack boat; looks just like 'em. I took a shot when I saw something move; didn't know it was a Terrestrial. Who are you? What you doin' here? We're pretty close to the edge of the oasis. That's Flap-jack country over there." He waved a hand toward the north, where the desert lay.

"I'm glad you're a poor shot. Some of those missiles were too close for comfort."

"Missiles, eh? Must be Flap-jack artillery. We got nothin' like that."

"I heard there was a full-fledged war brewing," said Retief. "I didn't expect—"

"Good!" Potter said. "We figured a few of you boys from Ivory would be joining up when you heard. You from Ivory?"

"Yes. I'm—"

"Hey, you must be Lemuel's cousin. Good night! I pretty near made a bad mistake. Lemuel's a tough man to explain anything to."

"I'm—"

"Keep your head down. These damn Flap-jacks have got some wicked hand weapons. Come on..." He began crawling through the brush. Retief followed. They crossed two hundred yards of rough country before Potter got to his feet, took out a soggy bandanna, and mopped his face.

"You move good for a city man. I thought you folks on Ivory just sat under those domes and read dials. But I guess bein' Lemuel's cousin—"

"As a matter of fact—"

"Have to get you some real clothes, though. Those city duds don't stand up on 'Dobe."

Retief looked down at his charred, torn, sweat-soaked powder-blue blazer and slacks, the informal uniform of a Third Secretary and Vice-Consul in the Corps Diplomatique Terrestrienne.

"This outfit seemed pretty rough-and-ready back home," he said. "But I guess leather has its points."

"Let's get on hack to camp. We'll just about make it by sundown. And look, don't say nothin' to Lemuel about me thinkin' you were, a Flap-jack."

I won t; but—

Potter was on his way, loping off up a gentle slope. Retief pulled off the sodden blazer, dropped it over a bush, added his string tie, and followed Potter.

"We're damn glad you're here, mister," said a fat man with two revolvers belted across his paunch. "We can use every man. We're in bad shape. We ran into the Flap-jacks three months ago and we haven't made a smart move since. First, we thought they were a native form we hadn't run into before. Fact is, one of the boys shot one, think it was fair game. I guess that was the start of it." He paused to stir the fire.

"And then a bunch of 'em hit Swazey's farm here. Killed two of his cattle, and pulled back," he said.

"We figure they thought the cows were people," said Swazey. "They were out for revenge."

"How could anybody think a cow was folks," another man put in. "They don't look nothin' like—"

"Don't be so dumb, Bert," said Swazey. "They'd never seen Terries before; they know better now."

Bert chuckled. "Sure do. We showed 'em the next time, didn't we, Potter? Got four—"

"They walked right up to my place a couple days after the first time," Swazey said. "We were ready for 'em. Peppered 'em good. They cut and run—"

"Flopped, you mean. Ugliest-lookin' critters you ever saw. Look just like a old piece of dirty blanket humpin' around.

"It's been goin' on this way ever since. They raid and then we raid. But lately they've been bringin' some big stuff into it. They've got some kind of pint-sized airships and automatic rifles. We've lost four men now and a dozen more in the freezer, waiting for the med ship. We can't afford it. The colony's got less than three hundred able-bodied men."

"But we're hangin' onto our farms," said Potter. "All these oases are old sea-beds—a mile deep, solid topsoil. And there's a couple of hundred others we haven't touched yet. The Flap-jacks won't get 'em while there's a man alive."

"The whole system needs the food we can raise," Bert said. "These farms we're tryin' to start won't be enough but they'll help."

"We been yellin' for help to the CDT, over on Ivory," said Potter. "But you know these Embassy stooges."

"We heard they were sendin' some kind of bureaucrat in here to tell us to get out and give the oasis to the Flap-jacks," said Swazey. He tightened his mouth. "We're waitin' for him…"

"Meanwhile we got reinforcements comin' up. We put out the word back home; we all got relatives on Ivory and Verde."

"Shut up, you damn fool!" a deep voice grated.

"Lemuel!" Potter said. "Nobody else could sneak up on us like that—"

"If I'd a been a Flap-jack, I'd of et you alive," the newcomer said, moving into the ring of the fire. He was a tall, broad-faced man in grimy leather. He eyed Retief.

"Who's that?"

"What do ya mean?" Potter spoke in the silence. "He's your cousin."

"He ain't no cousin of mine," Lemuel said. He stepped to Retief.

"Who you spyin' for, stranger?" he rasped.

Retief got to his feet. "I think I should explain—"

A short-nosed automatic appeared in Lemuel's hand, a clashing note against his fringed buckskins.

"Skip the talk. I know a fink when I see one."

"Just for a change, I'd like to finish a sentence," Retief said. "And I suggest you put your courage back in your pocket before it bites you."

"You talk too damned fancy to suit me."

"You're wrong. I talk to suit me. Now, for the last time: put it away."

Lemuel stared at Retief. "You givin' me orders…?"

Retief's left fist shot out and smacked Lemuel's face dead center. The raw-boned settler stumbled back, blood starting from his nose. The pistol fired into the dirt as he dropped it.

He caught himself, jumped for Retief...and met a straight right that snapped him onto his back-out cold.

"Wow!" said Potter. "The stranger took Lem...in two punches..."

"One," said Swazey. "That first one was just a love tap."

Bert froze. "Quiet, boys," he whispered. In the sudden silence a night lizard called. Retief strained, heard nothing. He narrowed his eyes, peering past the fire.

With a swift lunge he seized up the bucket of drinking water, dashed it over the fire, and threw himself flat. He heard the others hit the dirt a split second after him.

"You move fast for a city man," breathed Swazey beside him. "You see pretty good too. We'll split and take 'em from two sides. You and Bert from the left, me and Potter from the right."

"No," said Retief. "You wait here. I'm going out alone."

"What's the idea...?"

"Later. Sit tight and keep your eyes open." Retief took a bearing on a treetop faintly visible against the sky and started forward.

Five minutes' cautious progress brought Retief to a slight rise of ground. With infinite caution he raised himself and risked a glance over an outcropping of rock. The stunted trees ended just ahead. Beyond, he could make out the dim contour of rolling desert: Flap-jack country. He got to his feet, clambered over the stone, still hot after a day of tropical heat, and moved forward twenty yards. Around him he saw nothing but drifted sand, palely visible in the starlight, and the occasional shadow of jutting shale slabs. Behind him the jungle was still. He sat down on the ground to wait.

It was ten minutes before a movement caught his eye; something had separated itself from a dark mass of stone, and glided across a few yards of open ground to another shelter. Retief watched. Minutes passed. The shape moved again, slipped into a shadow ten feet distant. Retief felt the butt of the power pistol with his elbow. His guess had better be right...

There was a sudden rasp, like leather against concrete, and a flurry of sand as the Flap-jack charged. Retief rolled aside, then lunged, throwing his weight on the flopping Flap-jack— a yard square, three inches thick at the center, and all muscle. The ray-like creature heaved up, curled backward, its edge rippling, to stand on the flattened rim of its encircling sphincter. It scrabbled with its prehensile fringe-tentacles for a grip on Retief's shoulders. Retief wrapped his arms around the creature and struggled to his feet. The thing was heavy, a hundred pounds at least; fighting as it was, it seemed more like five hundred.

The Flap-jack reversed its tactics, becoming limp. Retief grabbed and felt a thumb slip into an orifice.

The creature went wild. Retief hung on, dug the thumb in deeper.

"Sorry, fellow," he muttered between his clenched teeth. "Eye-gouging isn't gentlemanly, but it's effective..."

The Flap-jack fell still; only its fringes rippling slowly. Retief relaxed the pressure of his thumb. The creature gave a tentative jerk; the thumb dug in. The Flap-jack went limp again, waiting.

"Now that we understand each other," said Retief, "lead me to your headquarters."

Twenty minutes' walk into the desert brought Retief to a low rampart of thorn branches: the Flap-jacks' outer defensive line against Terry forays. It would be as good a place as any to wait for the next move by the Flap-jacks. He sat down, eased the weight of his captive off his back, keeping a firm thumb in place. If his analysis of the situation was correct, a Flap-jack picket should be along before too long...

A penetrating beam of red light struck Retief in the face, then blinked off. He got to his feet. The captive Flap-jack rippled its fringe in an agitated way. Retief tensed his thumb.

"Sit tight," he said. "Don't try to do anything hasty..." His remarks were falling on deaf ears—or no ears at all—but the thumb spoke as loudly as words.

There was a slither of sand, then another. Retief became aware of a ring of presence's drawing closer.

Retief tightened his grip on the creature. He could see a dark shape now, looming up almost to his own six-three. It appeared that the Flap-jacks came in all sizes.

A low rumble sounded, like a deep-throated growl. It strummed on, then faded out. Retief cocked his head, frowning.

"Try it two octaves higher," he said.

"Awwrrp! Sorry. Is that better?" a clear voice came from the darkness.

'That's fine," Retief said. "I'm here to arrange an exchange of prisoners."

"Prisoners? But we have no prisoners."

"Sure you have. Me. Is it a deal?"

"Ah, yes, of course. Quite equitable. What guarantees do you require?"

"The word of a gentleman is sufficient." Retief released his captive. It flopped once and disappeared into the darkness.

"If you'd care to accompany me to our headquarters," the voice said, "we can discuss our mutual concerns in comfort."

"Delighted."

Red lights blinked briefly. Retief, glimpsing a gap in the thorny barrier, stepped through it. He followed dim shapes across warm sand to a low cave-like entry, faintly lit with a reddish glow.

"I must apologize for the awkward design of our comfort-dome," said the voice. "Had we known we would be honored by a visit."

"Think nothing of it," Retief said. "We diplomats are trained to crawl."

Inside, with knees bent and head ducked under the five-foot ceiling, Retief looked around at the walls of pink-toned nacre, a floor like burgundy-colored glass spread with silken rugs, and a low table of polished red granite set out with silver dishes and rose-crystal drinking tubes.

"Let me congratulate you," the voice said. Retief turned. An immense Flap-jack, hung with crimson trappings, rippled at his side. The voice issued from a disk strapped to its back. "Your skirmish-forms fight well. I think we will find in each other worthy adversaries."

'Thanks. I'm sure the test would be interesting, but I'm hoping we can avoid it."

"Avoid it?" Retief heard a low humming coming from the speaker in the silence. "Well, let us dine," the mighty Flapjack said at last, "we can resolve these matters later. I am called Hoshick of the Mosaic of the Two Dawns."

"I'm Retief." Hoshick waited expectantly. "...of the Mountain of Red Tape," Retief added.

"Take your place, Retief," said Hoshick. "I hope you won't find our rude couches uncomfortable." Two other large Flap-jacks came into the room and communed silently with Hoshick. "Pray forgive our lack of translating devices," he said to Retief. "Permit me to introduce my colleagues."

A small Flap-jack rippled into the chamber bearing on its back a silver tray, laden with aromatic food. The waiter served the diners and filled the drinking tubes with yellow wine.

"I trust you'll find these dishes palatable," Hoshick said.

"Our metabolisms are much alike, I believe." Retief tried the food; it had a delicious nut-like flavor. The wine was indistinguishable from Chateau d'Yquem.

"It was an unexpected pleasure to encounter your party here," Hoshick said. "I confess at first we took you for an indigenous earth-grubbing form, but we were soon disabused of that notion." He raised a tube, manipulating it deftly with his fringe tentacles. Retief returned the salute and drank.

"Of course," Hoshick continued, "as soon as we realized that you were sportsmen like ourselves, we attempted to make amends by providing a bit of activity for you. We've ordered out our heavier equipment and a few trained skirmishers and soon we'll be able to give you an adequate show, or so I hope."

"Additional skirmishers?" said Retief. "How many, if you don't mind my asking?"

"For the moment, perhaps only a few hundred. Thereafter...well, I'm sure we can arrange that between us. Personally I would prefer a contest of limited scope—no nuclear or radiation—effect weapons. Such a bore, screening the spawn for deviations. Though I confess we've come upon some remarkably useful sports: the ranger-form such as you made captive, for example. Simple-minded, of course, but a fantastically keen tracker."

"Oh, by all means," Retief said. "No atomics. As you pointed out, spawn-sorting is a nuisance, and then too, it's wasteful of troops."

"Ah, well, they are after all expendable. But we agree, no atomics. Have you tried the ground-gwack eggs? Rather a specialty of my Mosaic..."

"Delicious," said Retief. "I wonder if you've considered eliminating weapons altogether?"

A scratchy sound issued from the disk. "Pardon my laughter," Hoshick said, "but surely you jest?"

"As a matter of fact," said Retief, "we ourselves try to avoid the use of weapons."

"I seem to recall that our first contact of skirmish-forms involved the use of a weapon by one of your units."

"My apologies," said Retief. "The—ah—skirmish-form failed to recognize that he was dealing with a sportsman."

"Still, now that we have commenced so merrily with weapons..." Hoshick signaled and the servant refilled the drinking tubes.

"There is an aspect I haven't yet mentioned," Retief went on. "I hope you won't take this personally, but the fact is, our skirmish-forms think of weapons as something one employs only in dealing with certain specific life-forms."

"Oh? Curious. What forms are those?"

"Vermin. Deadly antagonists, but lacking in caste. I don't want our skirmish-forms thinking of such worthy adversaries as yourself as vermin."

"Dear me! I hadn't realized, of course. Most considerate of you to point it out." Hoshick clucked in dismay. "I see that skirmish-forms are much the same among you as with us: lacking in perception." He laughed scratchily.

"Which brings us to the crux of the matter," Retief said. "You see, we're up against a serious problem with regard to skirmish-forms: a low birth rate. Therefore we've reluctantly taken to substitutes for the mass actions so dear to the heart of the sportsman. We've attempted to put an end to these contests altogether..."

Hoshick coughed explosively, sending a spray of wine into the air. "What are you saying?" he gasped. "Are you proposing that Hoshick of the Mosaic of the Two Dawns abandon honor?"

"Sir!" said Retief sternly. "You forget yourself. I, Retief of the Red Tape, merely make an alternate proposal more in keeping with the newest sporting principles."

"New?" cried Hoshick. "My dear Retief, what a pleasant surprise! I'm enthralled with novel modes. One gets so out of touch. Do elaborate."

"It's quite simple, really. Each side selects a representative and the two individuals settle the issue between them."

"I...um...I'm afraid I don't understand. What possible significance could one attach to the activities of a couple of random skirmish-forms?"

"I haven't made myself clear," Retief said. He took a sip of wine. "We don't involve the skirmish-forms at all; that's quite passe."

"You don't mean...?"

"That's right. You and me."

Outside the starlit sand Retief tossed aside the power pistol and followed it with the leather shirt Swazey had lent him. By the faint light he could just make out the towering figure of the Flap-jack rearing up before him, his trappings gone. A silent rank of Flap-jack retainers were grouped behind him.

"I fear I must lay aside the translater now, Retief," said Hoshick. He sighed and rippled his fringe tentacles. "My spawn-fellows will never credit this. Such a curious turn fashion has taken. How much more pleasant it is to observe the action from a distance."

"I suggest we use Tennessee rules," said Retief. "They're very liberal: biting, gouging, stomping, kneeling, and, of course, choking, as well as the usual punching, shoving, and kicking."

"Hmmm. These gambits seem geared to forms employing rigid endoskeletons; I fear I shall be at a disadvantage."

"Of course," Retief said, "if you'd prefer a more plebeian type of contest…"

"By no means. But perhaps we could rule out tentacle-twisting, just to even the balance."

"Very well. Shall we begin?"

With a rush Hoshick threw himself at Retief, who ducked, whirled, and leaped on the Flap-jack's back—and felt himself flipped clear by a mighty ripple of the alien's slab-like body. Retief rolled aside as Hoshick turned on him, jumped to his feet, and threw a punch to Hoshick's mid-section. The alien whipped his left fringe around in an arc that connected with Retief's jaw, spinning onto his back. Hoshick's weight struck Retief like a dumptruck-load of concrete. Retief twisted, trying to roll. The flat body of the creature blanketed him. He worked an arm free and drummed blows on the leathery back. Hoshick nestled closer.

Retief's air was running out. He heaved up against the smothering weight; nothing budged. He was wasting his strength.

He remembered the ranger-form he had captured. The sensitive orifice had been placed ventrally, in what would be the thoracic area…

He groped, feeling tough hide set with horny granules. He would be missing skin tomorrow—if there was a tomorrow. His thumb found the orifice, and he probed.

The Flap-jack recoiled. Retief held fast, probed deeper, groping with the other hand. If the creature were bilaterally symmetrical there would be a set of ready-made handholds…

There were. Retief dug in and the Flap-jack writhed and pulled away. Retief held on, scrambled to his feet, threw his weight against Hoshick, and fell on top of him, still gouging. Hoshick rippled his fringe wildly, flopped in distress, then went limp. Retief relaxed, released his hold, and got to his feet, breathing hard. Hoshick humped himself over onto his ventral side, lifted, and moved gingerly over to the sidelines. His retainers came forward, assisted him into his trappings, and strapped on the translator. He sighed heavily, adjusting the volume.

"There is much to be said for the old system," he said. "What a burden one's sportsmanship places on one at times."

"Great fun, wasn't it?" said Retief. "Now, I know you'll be eager to continue. If you'll just wait while I run back and fetch some of our gouger-forms—"

"May hide-ticks devour the gouger-forms!" Hoshick bellowed. "You've given me such a sprong-ache as I'll remember each spawning-time for a year."

"Speaking of hide-ticks," said Retief, "we've developed a biter-form—"

"Enough!" Hoshick roared so loudly that the translator bounced on his hide. "Suddenly I yearn for the crowded yellow sands of Jaq. I had hoped..." He broke off, drawing a rasping breath. "I had hoped, Retief," he said, speaking sadly now, "to find a new land here where I might plan my own Mosaic, till these alien sands and bring forth such a crop of paradise-lichen as should glut the markets of a hundred worlds. But my spirit is not equal to the prospect of biter-forms and gouger-forms without end. I am shamed before you."

"To tell you the truth, I'm old-fashioned myself," said Retief. "I'd rather watch the action from a distance too."

"But surely your spawn-fellows would never condone such an attitude."

"My spawn-fellows aren't here. And besides, didn't I mention it? No one who's really in the know would think of engaging in competition by mere combat if there were any other way. Now, you mentioned tilling the sand, raising lichens—"

"That on which we dined," said Hoshick, "and from which the wine is made."

"The big trend in fashionable diplomacy today is farming competition. Now, if you'd like to take these deserts and raise lichen, we'll promise to stick to the oases and raise vegetables."

Hoshick curled his back in attention. "Retief, you're quite serious? You would leave all the fair sand hills to us?"

"The whole works, Hoshick. I'll take the oases."

Hoshick rippled his fringes ecstatically. "Once again you have outdone me, Retief," he cried, "this time, in generosity."

"We'll talk over the details later. I'm sure we can establish a set of rules that will satisfy all parties. Now I've got to get back. I think some of the gouger-forms are waiting to see me."

It was nearly dawn when Retief gave the whistled signal he had agreed on with Potter, then rose and walked into the, camp circle. Swazey stood up.

"There you are," he said, "We been wonderin' whether to go out after you."

Lemuel came forward, one eye black to the cheekbone. He held out a raw-boned hand. "Sorry I jumped you, stranger. Tell you the truth, I thought you was some kind of stool-pigeon from the CDT."

Bert came up behind Lemuel. "How do you know he ain't, Lemuel?" he said. "Maybe he——"

Lemuel floored Bert with a backward sweep of his arm. "Next cotton-picker says some embassy Johnny can cool me gets worse'n that."

"Tell me," said Retief. "How are you boys fixed for wine?"

"Wine? Mister, we been livin' on stump water for a year now. 'Dobe's fatal to the kind of bacteria it takes to ferment liquor."

"Try this." Retief handed over a squat jug. Swazey drew the cork, sniffed, drank, and passed it to Lemuel.

"Mister, where'd you get that?"

"The Flap-jacks make it. Here's another question for you: would you concede a share in this planet to the Flap-jacks in return for a peace guarantee?"

At the end of a half hour of heated debate Lemuel turned to Retief. "We'll make any reasonable deal," he said. "I guess they got as much right here as we have. I think we'd agree to a fifty-fifty split. That'd give about a hundred and fifty oases to each side."

"What would you say to keeping all the oases and giving them the desert?"

Lemuel reached for the wine jug, his eyes on Retief. "Keep talkin', mister," he said. "I think you got yourself a deal."

Consul Passwyn glanced up as Retief entered the office. "Sit down, Retief," he said absently. "I thought you were over on Pueblo, or Mud-flat, or whatever they call that desert.

"I'm back."

Passwyn eyed him sharply. "Well, well, what is it you need, man? Speak up. Don't expect me to request any military assistance."

Retief passed a bundle of documents across the desk.

"Here's the Treaty. And a Mutual Assistance Pact and a Trade Agreement."

"Eh?" Passwyn picked up the papers and rimed through them. He leaned back in his chair, beaming.

"Well, Retief, expeditiously handled." He stopped and blinked at the Vice-Consul. "You seem to have a bruise on your jaw. I hope you've been conducting yourself as befits a member of the Consulate staff."

"I attended a sporting event. One of the players got a little excited."

"Well…it's one of the hazards of the profession. One must pretend an interest in such matters." Passwyn rose and extended a hand. "You've done well, my boy. Let this teach you the value of following instructions to the letter."

Outside, by the hall incinerator drop, Retief paused long enough to take from his briefcase a large buff envelope, still sealed, and drop it in the slot.

* * * *

…Highly effective ancillary programs, developed early in Corps history, played a vital role in promoting harmony among the peace-loving peoples of the Galactic community. The notable success of Assistant Attaché (later Ambassador) Magnan in the cosmopolitization of reactionary elements in the Nicodeman Cluster was achieved through the agency of these enlightened programs…

Vol. III, reel 71 482 A. E. (AD 2943)

CULTURAL EXCHANGE

FIRST SECRETARY MAGNAN took his green-lined cape and orange-feathered beret from the clothes tree. "I'm off now, Retief," he said. "I hope you'll manage the administrative routine during my absence without any unfortunate incidents."

"That seems a modest enough hope," said Second Secretary Retief. "I'll try to live up to it."

"I don't appreciate frivolity with reference to this Division," Magnan said testily. "When I first came here, the Manpower Utilization Directorate, Division of Libraries and Education was a shambles. I fancy I've made MUDDLE what it is today. Frankly, I question the wisdom of placing you in charge of such a sensitive desk, even for two weeks; but remember, yours is a purely rubber-stamp function."

"In that case, let's leave it to Miss Furkle, and I'll take a couple of weeks off myself. With her poundage, she could bring plenty of pressure to bear."

"I assume you jest, Retief," Magnan said sadly. "I should expect even you to appreciate that Bogan participation in the Exchange Program may be the first step toward sublimation of their aggressions into more cultivated channels."

"I see they're sending two thousand students to d'Land," Retief said, glancing at the Memo for Record. "That's a sizable sublimation."

Magnan nodded. "The Bogans have launched no less than four military campaigns in the last two decades. They're known as the Hoodlums of the Nicodeman Cluster. Now, perhaps, we shall see them breaking that precedent and entering into the cultural life of the Galaxy."

"Breaking and entering," Retief said. "You may have something there. But I'm wondering what they'll study on d'Land. That's an industrial world of the poor-but-honest variety."

"Academic details are the affair of the students and their professors," Magnan said. "Our function is merely to bring them together. See that you don't antagonize the Bogan representative. This will be an excellent opportunity for you to practice your diplomatic restraint—not your strong point, I'm sure you'll agree—"

A buzzer sounded. Retief punched a button. "What is it, Miss Furkle?"

"That—bucolic person from Lovenbroy is here again."
On the small desk screen, Miss Furkle's meaty features were
compressed in disapproval.

"This fellow's a confounded pest; I'll leave him to you,
Retief," Magnan said. "Tell him something; get rid of him.
And remember: here at Corps HQ, all eyes are upon you."

"If I'd thought of that, I'd have worn my other suit,"
Retief said.

Magnan snorted and passed from view. Retief punched
Miss Furkle's button.

"Send the bucolic person in."

A tall broad man with bronze skin and grey hair, wearing
tight trousers of heavy cloth, a loose shirt open at the neck,
and a short jacket, stepped into the room, a bundle under his
arm. He paused at sight of Retief, looked him over
momentarily, then advanced and held out his hand. Retief
took it. For a moment the two big men stood, face to face.
The newcomer's jaw muscles knotted. Then he winced.
Retief dropped his hand, motioned to a chair.

"That's nice knuckle work, mister," the stranger said,
massaging his hand. "First time anybody ever did that to me.
My fault, though, I started it, I guess." He grinned and sat
down.

"What can I do for you?" the Second Secretary said. "My
name's Retief. I'm taking Mr. Magnan's place for a couple of
weeks."

"You work for this culture bunch, do you? Funny, I
thought they were all ribbon-counter boys. Never mind. I'm
Hank Arapoulous. I'm a farmer. What I wanted to see you
about was—" He shifted in his chair. "Well, out on
Lovenbroy we've got a serious problem. The wine crop is
just about ready. We start picking in another two, three
months. Now I don't know if you're familiar with the
Bacchus vines we grow?"

"No," Retief said. "Have a cigar?" He pushed a box across the desk. Arapoulous took one. "Bacchus vines are an unusual crop," he said, puffing life into the cigar. "Only mature every twelve years. In between, the vines don't need a lot of attention; our time's mostly our own. We like to farm, though. Spend a lot of time developing new forms. Apples the size of a melon—and sweet."

"Sounds very pleasant," Retief said. "Where does the Libraries and Education Division come in?"

Arapoulous leaned forward. "We go in pretty heavy for the arts. Folks can't spend all their time hybridizing plants. We've turned all the land area we've got into parks and farms; course, we left some sizable forest areas for hunting and such. Lovenbroy's a nice place, Mr. Retief."

"It sounds like it, Mr. Arapoulous. Just what—"

"Call me Hank. We've got long seasons back home. Five of 'em. Our year's about eighteen Terry months. Cold as hell in winter—eccentric orbit, you know. Blue-black sky, stars visible all day. We do mostly painting and sculpture in the winter. Then Spring—still plenty cold. Lots of skiing, bobsledding, ice skating—and it's the season for woodworkers. Our furniture—"

"I've seen some of your furniture, I believe," said Retief. "Beautiful work."

Arapoulous nodded. "All local timbers, too. Lots of metals in our soil; those sulphates give the woods some color, I'll tell you. Then comes the Monsoon. Rain—it comes down in sheets—but the sun's gettin' closer; shines all the time. Ever seen it pouring rain in the sunshine? That's the music-writing season. Then summer. Summer's hot. We stay inside in the daytime, and have beach parties all night. Lots of beach on Lovenbroy, we're mostly islands. That's the drama and symphony time. The theatres are set up on the sand, or anchored on barges off-shore. You have the music and the surf and the bonfires and stars—we're close to the center of a globular cluster, you know…"

"You say it's time now for the wine crop?"

"That's right. Autumn's our harvest season. Most years we have just the ordinary crops: fruit, grain, that kind of thing. Getting it in doesn't take long. We spend most of the time on architecture, getting new places ready for the winter, or remodeling the older ones. We spend a lot of time in our houses; we like to have them comfortable. But this year's different. This is Wine Year."

Arapoulous puffed on his cigar and looked worriedly at Retief. "Our wine crop is our big money crop," he said. "We make enough to keep us going. But this year…"

"The crop isn't panning out?"

"Oh, the crop's fine; one of the best I can remember.

Course, I'm only twenty-eight; I can't remember but two other harvests. The problem's not the crop…"

"Have you lost your markets? That sounds like a matter for the Commercial—"

"Lost our markets? Mister, nobody that ever tasted our wines ever settled for anything else!"

"It sounds like I've been missing something," said Retief. "I'll have to try them some time."

Arapoulous put his bundle on the desk, pulled off the wrappings. "No time like the present," he said.

Retief looked at the two squat bottles, one green, one amber, both dusty, with faded labels, and blackened corks secured by wire.

"Drinking on duty is frowned on in the Corps, Mr. Arapoulous," he said.

"This isn't drinking, it's just wine." Arapoulous pulled the wire retainer loose and thumbed the cork. It rose slowly, then popped in the air. Arapoulous caught it. Aromatic fumes wafted from the bottle. "Besides, my feelings would be hurt if you didn't join me." He winked.

Retief took two thin-walled glasses from a table beside the desk. "Come to think of it, we also have to be careful about violating quaint native customs." Arapoulous filled the glasses. Retief picked one up, sniffed the deep rust colored fluid, tasted it, then took a healthy swallow. He looked at Arapoulous thoughtfully.

"Hmmm, it tastes like salted pecans, with an undercurrent of crusted port."

"Don't try to describe it, Mr. Retief," Arapoulous said. He took a mouthful of wine, swished it around his teeth, and swallowed. "It's Bacchus wine, that's all." He pushed the second bottle toward Retief. "The custom back home is to alternate red wine and black."

Retief put aside his cigar, pulled the wires loose, nudged the cork, and caught it as it popped up.

"Bad luck if you miss the cork," Arapoulous said, nodding. "You probably never heard about the trouble we had on Lovenbroy a few years back?"

"Can't say that I did, Hank." Retief poured the black wine into the two fresh glasses. "Here's to the harvest."

"We've got plenty of minerals on Lovenbroy," Arapoulous said, swallowing wine. "But we don't plan to wreck the landscape mining 'em. We like to farm. About ten years back some neighbors of ours landed a force. They figured they knew better what to do with our minerals than we did. Wanted to strip-mine, smelt ore. We convinced 'em otherwise. But it took a year, and we lost a lot of men."

"That's too bad,'" Retief said. "I'd say this one tastes more like roast beef and popcorn over a Riesling base."

"It put us in a bad spot," Arapoulous went on. "We had to borrow money from a world called Croanie, mortgaged our crops; we had to start exporting art work too. Plenty of buyers, but it's not the same when you're doing it for strangers."

"What's the problem?" Retief said, "Croanie about to foreclose?"

"The loan's due. The wine crop would put us in the clear; but we need harvest hands. Picking Bacchus grapes isn't a job you can turn over to machinery—and we wouldn't if we could. Vintage season is the high point of living on Lovenbroy. Everybody joins in. First, there's the picking in the fields. Miles and miles of vineyards covering the mountain sides, crowding the river banks, with gardens here and there. Big vines, eight feet high, loaded with fruit, and deep grass growing between. The wine-carriers keep on the run, bringing wine to the pickers. There's prizes for the biggest day's output, bets on who can fill the most baskets in an hour. The sun's high and bright, and it's just cool enough to give you plenty of energy. Come nightfall the tables are set up in the garden plots, and the feast is laid on: roast turkeys, beef, hams, all kinds of fowl. Big salads and plenty of fruit and fresh-baked bread…and wine, plenty of wine. The cooking's done by a different crew each night in each garden, and there's prizes for the best crews.

"Then the wine-making. We still tramp out the vintage. That's mostly for the young folks—but anybody's welcome. That's when things start to get loosened up. Matter of fact, pretty near half our young-uns are born about nine months after a vintage. All bets are off then. It keeps a fellow on his toes though; ever tried to hold onto a gal wearin' nothing but a layer of grape juice?"

"Never did," Retief said. "You say most of the children are born after a vintage. That would make them only twelve years old by the time—"

"Oh, that's Lovenbroy years; they'd be eighteen, Terry reckoning."

"I was thinking you looked a little mature for twenty-eight," Retief said.

"Forty-two, Terry years," Arapoulous said. "But this year—it looks bad. We've got a bumper crop—and we're short-handed. If we don't get a big vintage, Croanie steps in; lord knows what they'll do to the land.

"What we figured was, maybe you Culture boys could help us out: a loan to see us through the vintage, enough to hire extra hands. Then we'd repay it in sculpture, painting, furniture—"

"Sorry, Hank. All we do here is work out itineraries for traveling sideshows, that kind of thing. Now if you needed a troop of Groaci nose-flute players—"

"Can they pick grapes?"

"Nope—anyway they can't stand the daylight. Have you talked this over with the Labor office?"

"Sure did. They said they'd fix us up with all the electronics specialists and computer programmers we wanted—but no field hands. Said it was what they classified as menial drudgery; you'd have thought I was trying to buy slaves."

The buzzer sounded. Miss Furkle appeared on the desk screen.

"You're due at the Inter-Group Council in five minutes," she said. "Then afterwards, there are the Bogan students to meet."

"Thanks." Retief finished his glass and stood. "I have to run, Hank," he said. "Let me think this over. Maybe I can come up with something. Check with me day after tomorrow. And you'd better leave the bottles here. Cultural exhibits, you know.

As the council meeting broke up, Retief caught the eye of a colleague across the table.

"Mr. Whaffle, you mentioned a shipment going to a place called Croanie. What are they getting?"

Whaffle blinked. "You're the fellow who's filling in for Magnan, over at MUDDLE," he said. "Properly speaking, equipment grants are the sole concern of the Motorized Equipment Depot, Division of Loans and Exchanges." He pursed his lips. "However, I suppose there's no harm in my telling you. They'll be receiving heavy mining equipment."

"Drill rigs, that sort of thing?"

"Strip mining gear." Whaffle took a slip of paper from a breast pocket and blinked at it. "Bolo Model WV/1 tractors, to be specific. Why MUDDLE's interest in MEDDLE's activities?"

"Forgive my curiosity, Mr. Whaffle. It's just that Croanie cropped up earlier today; seems she holds a mortgage on some vineyards over on—"

"That's not MEDDLE's affair, sir," Whaffle cut in. "I have sufficient problems as Chief of MEDDLE without probing into MUDDLE's business."

"Speaking of tractors," another man put in, "we over at the Special Committee for Rehabilitation and Overhaul of Underdeveloped Nations' General Economies have been trying for months to get a request for mining equipment for d'Land through MEDDLE—"

"SCROUNGE was late on the scene," Whaffle said. "First come, first served, that's our policy at MEDDLE. Good day, gentlemen." He strode off, a briefcase under his arm.

"That's the trouble with peaceful worlds," the SCROUNGE committeeman said. "Boge is a trouble-maker, so every agency in the Corps is out to pacify her, while my chance to make a record—that is, assist peace-loving d'Land, comes to nought."

"What kind of university do they have on d'Land?" asked Retief. "We're sending them two thousand exchange students. It must be quite an institution—"

"University? D'Land has one under-endowed technical college."

"Will all the exchange students be studying at the Technical College?"

"Two thousand students? Hah! Two hundred students would overtax the facilities of the college!"

"I wonder if the Bogans know that?"

"The Bogans? Why, most of d'Land's difficulties are due to the unwise trade agreement she entered into with Boge. Two thousand students indeed." He snorted and walked away.

Retief stopped by the office to pick up his short violet cape, then rode the elevator to the roof of the 230-story Corps HQ building and hailed a cab to the port. The Bogan students had arrived early. Retief saw them lined up on the ramp waiting to go through customs. It would be half an hour before they were cleared through. He turned into the bar and ordered a beer. A tall young fellow on the next stool raised his glass.

"Happy days," he said.

"And nights to match."

"You said it." He gulped half his beer. "My name's Karsh. Mr. Karsh. Yep, Mr. Karsh. Boy, this is a drag, sitting around this place waiting."

"You meeting somebody?"

"Yeah. Bunch of babies. Kids. How they expect—Never mind. Have one on me."

"Thanks. You a scoutmaster?"

"I'll tell you what I am; I'm a cradle-robber. You know," he turned to Retief, "not one of those kids is over eighteen."

He hiccuped. "Students, you know. Never saw a student with a beard, did you?"

"Lots of times. You're meeting the students, are you?"

The young fellow blinked at Retief. "Oh, you know about it, huh?"

"I represent MUDDLE."

Karsh finished his beer and ordered another. "I came on ahead: sort of an advance guard for the kids. I trained 'em myself. Treated it like a game, but they can handle a CSU. Don't know how they'll act under pressure. If I had my old platoon—"

He looked at his beer glass, then pushed it back. "Had enough," he said. "So long, friend. Or are you coming along?"

Retief nodded. "Might as well."

At the exit to the Customs enclosure, Retief watched as the first of the Bogan students came through, caught sight of Karsh, and snapped to attention.

"Drop that, mister," Karsh snapped. "Is that any way for a student to act?"

The youth, a round-faced lad with broad shoulders, grinned.

"Guess not," he said. "Say, uh, Mr. Karsh, are we gonna get to go to town. Us fellas were thinkin'—"

"You were, hah? You act like a bunch of school kids—I mean... No! Now line up!"

"We have quarters ready for the students," Retief said.

"If you'd like to bring them around to the west side, I have a couple of copters laid on."

"Thanks," said Karsh. "They'll stay here until take-off time. Can't have the little darlings wandering around loose. Might get ideas about going over the hill." He hiccuped. "I mean, they might play hookey."

"We've scheduled your re-embarkation for noon tomorrow. That's a long wait. MUDDLE's arranged theatre tickets and a dinner."

"Sorry," Karsh said. "As soon as the baggage gets here, we're off." He hiccuped again. "Can't travel without our baggage, y know.

"Suit yourself," Retief said. "Where's the baggage now?"

"Coming in aboard a Croanie lighter."

"Maybe you'd like to arrange for a meal for the students here?"

"Sure," Karsh said. "That's a good idea. Why don't you join us?" Karsh winked. "And bring a few beers."

"Not this time," Retief said. He watched the students, still emerging from Customs. "They seem to be all boys," he commented. "No female students?"

"Maybe later," Karsh said, "after we see how the first bunch is received."

Back at the MUDDLE office, Retief buzzed Miss Furkle. "Do you know the name of the institution these Bogan students are bound for?"

"Why, the university at d'Land, of course."

"Would that be the Technical College?"

Miss Furkle's mouth puckered. "I'm sure I've never pried into these details—"

"Where does doing your job stop and prying begin, Miss Furkle?" Retief said. "Personally, I'm curious as to just what it is these students are travelling so far to study—at Corps expense."

"Mr. Magnan never—"

"For the present, Miss Furkle, Mr. Magnan is vacationing. That leaves me with the question of two thousand young male students headed for a world with no classrooms for them...a world in need of tractors. But the tractors are on their way to Croanie, a world under obligations to Boge. And

Croanie holds a mortgage on the best grape acreage on Lovenbroy."

"Well!" Miss Furkle snapped, her small eyes glaring under unplucked brows. "I hope you're not questioning Mr. Magnan's wisdom!"

"About Mr. Magnan's wisdom there can be no doubts," Retief said. "But never mind. I'd like you to look up an item for me. How many tractors will Croanie be getting under the MEDDLE program?"

"Why, that's entirely MUDDLE business," Miss Furkle said, "Mr. Magnan always—"

"I'm sure he did. Let me know about the tractors as soon as you can."

Miss Furkle sniffed and disappeared from the screen. Retief left the office, descended forty-one stories, and followed a corridor to the Corps Library. In the stacks he thumbed through catalogs and pored over indices.

"Can I help you?" someone chirped. A tiny librarian stood at his elbow.

"Thank you, Ma'am," Retief said. "I'm looking for information on a mining rig: a Bolo model WV tractor."

"You won't find it in the industrial section," the librarian said. "Come along." Retief followed her along the stacks to a well-lit section lettered ARMAMENTS. She took a tape from the shelf, plugged it into the viewer, flipped through, and stopped at a picture of a squat armored vehicle.

"That's the model WV," she said. "It's what is known as a Continental Siege Unit. It carries four men, with a half-megaton/second firepower—"

"There must be an error somewhere," Retief said. "The Bolo model I want is a tractor, model WV M-l-"

"Oh, the modification was the addition of a blade for demolition work. That must be what confused you."

"Probably—among other things. Thank you."

Miss Furkle was waiting at the office. "I have the information you wanted," she said. "I've had it for over ten minutes. I was under the impression you needed it urgently, and I went to great lengths—"

"Sure," Relief said. "Shoot. How many tractors?"

"Five hundred."

"Are you sure?"

Miss Furkle's chins quivered. "Well! If you feel I'm incompetent."

"Just questioning the possibility of a mistake, Miss Furkle. Five hundred tractors is a lot of equipment."

"Was there anything further?" Miss Furkle inquired frigidly.

"I sincerely hope not," Relief said.

Leaning back in Magnan's padded chair with its power swivel and hip-u-matic contour, Retief leafed through a folder labeled "CERP 7-602-Ba; CROANIE (general)." He paused at a page headed INDUSTRY. Still reading, he opened the desk drawer, took out the two bottles of Bacchus wine and two glasses. He poured an inch of wine into each, then sipped the black wine meditatively. It would be a pity, he reflected, if anything should interfere with the production of such vintages…

Half an hour later he laid the folder aside, keyed the phone, and put through a call to the Croanie Legation, asking for the Commercial attaché.

"Retief here, Corps HQ," he said airily. "About the MEDDLE shipment, the tractors. I'm wondering if there's been a slip-up. My records show we're shipping five hundred units."

"That's correct. Five hundred."

Retief waited.

"Ah…are you there, Mr. Retief?"

"I'm still here. And I'm still wondering about the five hundred tractors."

"It's perfectly in order; I thought it was all settled. Mr. Whaffle—"

"One unit would require a good-sized planet to handle its output," Retief said. "Now Croanie subsists on her fisheries. She has perhaps half-a-dozen pint-sized processing plants. Maybe, in a bind, they could handle the ore ten WV's could scrape up...if Croanie had any ore. By the way, isn't a WV a poor choice as a mining outfit? I should think—"

"See here, Retief, why all this interest in a few surplus tractors? And in any event, what business is it of yours how we plan to use the equipment? That's an internal affair of my government. Mr. Whaffle—"

"I'm not Mr. Whaffle. What are you going to do with the other four hundred and ninety tractors?"

"I understood the grant was to be with no strings attached!"

"I know it's bad manners to ask questions. It's an old diplomatic tradition that any time you can get anybody to accept anything as a gift, you've scored points in the game. But if Croanie has some scheme cooking—"

"Nothing like that, Retief! It's a mere business transaction."

"What kind of business do you do with a Bolo WV? With or without a blade attached, it's what's known as a continental siege unit—"

"Great Heavens, Retief! Don't jump to conclusions! Would you have us branded as warmongers? Frankly—is this a closed line?"

"Certainly. You may speak freely."

"The tractors are for trans-shipment. We've gotten ourselves into a difficult situation in our balance of payments.

This is an accommodation to a group with which we have strong business ties."

"I understand you hold a mortgage on the best land on Lovenbroy," Retief said. "Any connection?"

"Why...ah...no. Of course not."

"Who gets the tractors eventually?"

"Retief, this is unwarranted interference—"

"Who gets them?"

"They happen to be going to Lovenbroy. But I scarcely see—"

"And who's the friend you're helping out with an unauthorized trans-shipment of grant material?"

"Why...ah...I've been working with a Mr. Gulver, a Bogan representative."

"And when will they be shipped?"

"Why, they went out a week ago. They'll be halfway there by now. But look here, Retief, this isn't what you're thinking!"

"How do you know what I'm thinking? I don't know myself." Retief rang off and buzzed the secretary.

"Miss Furkle, I'd like to be notified immediately of any new applications that might come in from the Bogan Consulate for placement of students."

"Well, it happens, by coincidence, that I have an application here now. Mr. Gulver of the Consulate brought it in."

"Is Mr. Gulver in the office? I'd like to see him."

"I'll ask him if he has time."

It was half a minute before a thick-necked red-faced man in a tight hat walked in. He wore an old-fashioned suit, a drab shirt, shiny shoes with round toes, and an ill-tempered expression.

"What is it you wish?" he barked. "I understood in my discussions with the other...ah...civilian there'd be no further need for these irritating conferences."

"I've just learned you're placing more students abroad, Mr. Gulver. How many this time?"

"Three thousand."

"And where will they be going?"

"Croanie—it's all in the application form I've handed in. Your job is to provide transportation."

"Will there be any other students embarking this season?"

"Why...perhaps. That's Boge's business." Gulver looked at Retief with pursed lips. "As a matter of fact, we had in mind dispatching another two thousand to Featherweight."

"Another under-populated world—and in the same cluster, I believe," Retief said. "Your people must be unusually interested in that region of space."

"If that's all you wanted to know, I'll be on my way. I have matters of importance to see to."

After Gulver left Retief called Miss Furkle in. "I'd like to have a break-out of all the student movements that have been planned under the present program," he said. "And see if you can get a summery of what MEDDLE has been shipping lately."

Miss Furkle bridled. "If Mr. Magnan were here, I'm sure he wouldn't dream of interfering in the work of other departments. I...overheard your conversation with the gentleman from the Croanie Legation—"

"The lists, Miss Furkle."

"I'm not accustomed," Miss Furkle said, "to intruding in matters outside our interest cluster."

"That's worse than listening in on phone conversations, eh? But never mind. I need the information, Miss Furkle."

"Loyalty to my Chief—"

"Loyalty to your pay-check should send you scuttling for the material I've asked for," Retief said. "I'm taking full responsibility. Now scat."

The buzzer sounded. Retief flipped a key. "MUDDLE, Retief speaking…"

Arapoulous' brown face appeared on the desk screen.

"How do, Retief. Okay if I come up?"

"Sure, Hank. I want to talk to you."

In the office, Arapoulous took a chair. "Sorry if I'm rushing you," he said. "But have you got anything for me?"

Retief waved at the wine bottles. "What do you know about Croanie?"

"Croanie? Not much of a place. Mostly ocean. All right if you like fish, I guess. We import some seafood from there. Nice prawns in monsoon time. Over a foot long."

"You on good terms with them?"

"Sure, I guess so. Course, they're pretty thick with Boge."

"So?"

"Didn't I tell you? Boge was the bunch that tried to take us over here a dozen years back. They would have made it, too, if they hadn't had a lot of bad luck. Their armor went in the drink, and without armor they're easy game."

Miss Furkle buzzed. "I have your lists," she said shortly.

"Bring them in, please."

The secretary placed the papers on the desk. Arapoulous caught her eye and grinned. She sniffed and marched from the room.

"What she needs is a slippery time in the grape mash," Arapoulous observed. Retief thumbed through the papers, pausing to read here and there. He finished and looked at Arapoulous.

"How many men do you need for the harvest, Hank?" Retief inquired.

Arapoulous sniffed his wine glass.

"A hundred would help," he said. "'A thousand would be better. Cheers."

"What would you say to two thousand?"

"Two thousand? Retief, you're not foolin'?"

"I hope not." He picked up the phone, called the Port Authority, and asked for the dispatch clerk.

"Hello, Jim. Say, I have a favor to ask of you. You know that contingent of Bogan students; they're travelling aboard the two CDT transports. I'm interested in the baggage that goes with the students. Has it arrived yet? Okay, I'll wait..."

Jim came back to the phone. "Yeah, Retief, it's here. Just arrived. But there's a funny thing. It's not consigned to d'Land; it's ticketed clear through to Lovenbroy."

"Listen, Jim," Retief said. "I want you to go over to the warehouse and take a look at that baggage for me."

Retief waited while the dispatch clerk carried out the errand. The level in the two bottles had gone down an inch when Jim returned to the phone.

"Hey, I took a look at that baggage, Retief. Something funny going on. Guns. 2nn needlers, Mark XII hand blasters, power pistols—"

"It's okay, Jim. Nothing to worry about. Just a mix-up. Now, Jim, I'm going to ask you to do something more for me. I'm covering for a friend; it seems he slipped up. I wouldn't want word to get out, you understand. I'll send along a written change order in the morning that will cover you officially. Meanwhile, here's what I want you to do..."

Retief gave instructions, then rang off and turned to Arapoulous.

"As soon as I get off a couple of TWX's, we'd better get down to the port, Hank. I think I'd like to see the students off personally."

Karsh met Retief as he entered the Departures enclosure at the port.

"What's going on here?" he demanded. "There's some funny business with my baggage consignment; they won't let me see it. I've got a feeling it's not being loaded."

"You'd better hurry, Mr. Karsh," Retief said. "You're scheduled to blast off in less than an hour. Are the students all loaded?"

"Yes, blast you! What about my baggage? Those vessels aren't moving without it!"

"No need to get so upset about a few toothbrushes, is there, Mr. Karsh?" Retief said blandly. "Still, if you're worried—" He turned to Arapoulous.

"Hank, why don't you walk Mr. Karsh over to the warehouse and...ah...take care of him?"

"I know just how to handle it," Arapoulous said.

The dispatch clerk came up to Retief. "I caught the tractor shipment," he said. "Funny kind of mistake, but it's okay now. They're being off-loaded at d'Land. I talked to the traffic controller there; he said they weren't looking for any students."

"The labels got switched, Jim. The students go where the baggage was consigned; too bad about the mistake there, but the Armaments Office will have a man along in a little while to dispose of the guns. Keep an eye out for the real luggage; no telling where it's gotten to—"

"Here!" a hoarse voice yelled. Retief turned. A disheveled figure in a tight hat was crossing the enclosure, his arms waving.

"Hi there, Mr. Gulver," Retief called. "How's Boge's business coming along?"

"Piracy!" Gulver blurted as he came up to Retief. "You've got a hand in this, I don't doubt! Where's that Magnan fellow..."

"What seems to be the problem?" Retief said.

"Hold those transports! I've just been notified that the baggage shipment has been impounded. I'll remind you, that shipment enjoys diplomatic free entry."

"Who told you it was impounded?"

"Never mind! I have my sources!"

Two tall men buttoned into grey tunics came up. "Are you Mr. Retief of CDT?" one said.

"That's right."

"What about my baggage!" Gulver cut in. "And I'm warning you, if those ships lift without—"

"These gentlemen are from the Armaments Control Commission," Retief said. "Would you like to come along and claim your baggage, Mr. Gulver?"

"From what? I..." Gulver turned two shades redder about the ears. "Armaments...?"

"The only shipment I've held up seems to be somebody's arsenal," Retief said. "Now, if you claim this is your baggage..."

"Why, impossible," Gulver said in a strained voice. "Armaments? Ridiculous. There's been an error."

At the baggage warehouse, Gulver looked glumly at the opened cases of guns. "No, of course not," he said dully. "Not my baggage. Not my baggage at all."

Arapoulous appeared, supporting the stumbling figure of Mr. Karsh.

"What—what's this?" Gulver spluttered. "Karsh? What's happened...?"

"He had a little fall. He'll be okay," Arapoulous said.

"You'd better help him to the ship," Retief said. "It's ready to lift. We wouldn't want him to miss it."

"Leave him to me!" Gulver snapped, his eyes slashing at Karsh. "I'll see he's dealt with."

"I couldn't think of it," Retief said. "He's a guest of the Corps, you know. We'll see him safely aboard."

Gulver turned and signaled frantically. Three heavyset men in identical drab suits detached themselves from the wall and crossed to the group.

"Take this man," Gulver snapped, indicating Karsh, who looked at him dazedly.

"We take our hospitality seriously," Retief said. "We'll see him aboard the vessel."

Gulver opened his mouth—

"I know you feel bad about finding guns instead of school books in your luggage," Retief said, looking Gulver in the eye. "You'll be busy straightening out the details of the mix-up. You'll want to avoid further complications."

"Ah...yes," Gulver said.

Arapoulous went on to the passenger conveyor, then turned to wave.

"Your man—he's going too?" Gulver blurted.

"He's not our man, properly speaking," Retief said. He lives on Lovenbroy."

"Lovenbroy?" Gulver choked. "But...the...I..."

"I know you said the students were bound for d'Land," Retief said. "But I guess that was just another aspect of the general confusion. The course plugged into the navigators was to Lovenbroy. You'll be glad to know they're still headed there—even without the baggage."

"Perhaps," Gulver said grimly, "perhaps they'll manage without it."

"By the way," Retief said. "There was another funny mix-up. There were some tractors—for industrial use, you'll recall. I believe you co-operated with Croanie in arranging the grant through MEDDLE. They were erroneously consigned to Lovenbroy, a purely agricultural world. I saved you some embarrassment, I trust, Mr. Gulver, by arranging to have them off-loaded at d'Land."

"D'Land! You've put the CSU's in the hands of Boge's bitterest enemies...?"

"But they're only tractors, Mr. Gulver. Peaceful devices. Isn't that correct?"

"That's...correct." Gulver sagged. Then he snapped erect. "Hold the ships!" he yelled. "I'm canceling the student exchange."

His voice was drowned by the rumble as the first of the monster transports rose from the launch pit, followed a moment later by the second. Retief watched them fade out of sight, then turned to Gulver.

"They're off," he said. "Let's hope they get a liberal education."

Retief lay on his back in deep grass by a stream, eating grapes. A tall figure, appearing on the knoll above him, waved.

"Retief!" Hank Arapoulous bounded down the slope. "I heard you were here—and I've got news for you. You won the final day's picking competition. Over two hundred bushels! That's a record! Let's get on over to the garden, shall we? Sounds like the celebration's about to start."

In the flower-crowded park among the stripped vines, Retief and Arapoulous made their way to a laden table under the lanterns. A tall girl dressed in a loose white garment, with long golden hair, came up to Arapoulous.

"Delinda, this is Retief—today's winner. And he's also the fellow that got those workers for us."

Delinda smiled at Retief. "I've heard about you, Mr. Retief. We weren't sure about the boys at first; two thousand Bogans, and all confused about baggage that went astray. But they seemed to like the picking..." She smiled again.

"That's not all; our gals liked the boys," Hank said. "Even Bogans aren't so bad, minus their irons. A lot of 'em will be staying on. But how come you didn't tell me you were coming, Retief? I'd have laid on some kind of big welcome."

"I liked the welcome I got. And I didn't have much notice. Mr. Magnan was a little upset when he got back. It seems I exceeded my authority."

Arapoulous laughed. "I had a feeling you were wheelin' pretty free, Retief. I hope you didn't get into any trouble over it."

"No trouble," Retief said. "A few people were a little unhappy with me. It seems I'm not ready for important assignments at Departmental level. I was shipped off here to the boondocks to get a little more field experience."

"Delinda, look after Retief," said Arapoulous. "I'll see you later. I've got to see to the wine judging." He disappeared in the crowd.

"Congratulations on winning the day," said Delinda. "I noticed you at work. You were wonderful. I'm glad you're going to have the prize."

"Thanks. I noticed you too, flitting around in that white nightie of yours. But why weren't you picking grapes with the rest of us?"

"I had a special assignment."

"Too bad. You should have had a chance at the prize."

Delinda took Retief's hand. "I wouldn't have anyway," she said. "I'm the prize."

...Supplementing broad knowledge of affairs with such shrewd gambits as identification with significant local groups, and the consequent deft manipulating of inter-group rivalries, Corps officials on the scene played decisive roles in the preservation of domestic tranquility on many a far-flung world. At Fust, Ambassador Magnan forged to the van in the exercise of the technique...

Vol VII, reel 43. 487 A. E. (AD 2948)

AIDE MEMOIRE

ACROSS THE TABLE from Retief, Ambassador Magnan, rustling a stiff sheet of parchment, looked grave.

"This *aide memoire,*" he said, "was just handed to me by the Cultural Attaché. It's the third on the subject this week. It refers to the matter of sponsorship of Youth groups."

"Some youths," Retief said. "Average age: seventy-five."

"The Fustians are a long-lived people," Magnan snapped. "These matters are relative. At seventy-five, a male Fustian is at a trying age."

"That's right; he'll try anything in the hope it will maim somebody."

"Precisely the problem," Magnan replied. "But the Youth Movement is the important news in today's political situation here on Fust, and sponsorship of Youth groups is a shrewd stroke on the part of the Terrestrial Embassy. At my suggestion, well nigh every member of the mission has leaped at the opportunity to score a few p— that is, to cement relations with this emergent power group: the leaders of the future. You, Retief, as Counselor, are the outstanding exception."

"I'm not convinced these hoodlums need my help in organizing their rumbles," Retief said. "Now, if you have a proposal for a pest control group—"

"To the Fustians, this is no jesting matter," Magnan cut in. "This group," he glanced at the paper, "known as the Sexual, Cultural and Athletic Recreational Society, or SCARS, for short, has been awaiting sponsorship for a matter of weeks now."

"Meaning they want someone to buy them a clubhouse, uniforms, equipment, and anything else they need to plot against the peace in style," Retief said.

"If we don't act promptly, the Groaci embassy may well anticipate us. They're very active here."

"That's an idea," said Retief, "let 'em. After a while they'll be broke—instead of us."

"Nonsense. The group requires a sponsor. I can't actually order you to step forward. However..." Magnan let the sentence hang in the air. Retief raised one eyebrow.

"For a minute there," he said, "I thought you were going to make a positive statement."

Magnan leaned back, lacing his fingers over his stomach. "I don't think you'll find a diplomat of my experience doing anything so naive," he said.

"I like the adult Fustians," said Retief. "Too bad they have to lug half a ton of horn around on their backs. I wonder if surgery—"

"Great heavens, Retief," Magnan spluttered. "I'm amazed that even you would bring up a matter of such delicacy. A race's unfortunate physical characteristics are hardly a fit matter for Terrestrial curiosity."

"Well, I've only been here a month. But it's been my experience, Mr. Ambassador, that few people are above improving on nature; otherwise you, for example, would be tripping over your beard."

Magnan shuddered. "Please—never mention the idea to a Fustian."

Retief stood. "My own program for the day includes going over to the dockyards. There are some features of this new passenger liner the Fustians are putting together that I want to look into. With your permission, Mr. Ambassador...?"

Magnan snorted. "Your preoccupation with the trivial disturbs me, Retief. More interest in substantive matters— such as working with youth groups—would create a far better impression."

"Before getting too involved with these groups, it might be a good idea to find out a little more about them," Retief said. "Who organizes them? There are three strong political parties here on Fust; what's the alignment of this SCARS organization?"

"You forget, these are merely teen-agers, so to speak," Magnan said. "Politics mean nothing to them...yet."

"Then there are the Groaci. Why their passionate interest in a two-horse world like Fust? Normally they're concerned with nothing but business; and what has Fust got that they could use?

"You may rule out the commercial aspect in this instance," said Magnan. "Fust possesses a vigorous steel-age manufacturing economy. The Groaci are barely ahead of them."

"Barely," said Retief. "Just over the line into crude atomics...like fission bombs."

Magnan, shaking his head, turned back to his papers. "What market exists for such devices on a world at peace?" he said. "I suggest you address your attention to the less spectacular but more rewarding work of insinuating yourself into the social patterns of the local youth."

"I've considered the matter," Retief said, "and before I meet any of the local youth socially I want to get myself a good blackjack."

Retief left the sprawling bungalow-type building that housed the chancery of the Terrestrial Embassy, hailed one of the ponderous slow-moving Fustian flat-cars, and leaned back against the wooden guard rail as the heavy vehicle trundled through the city toward the looming gantries of the shipyards. It was a cool morning with a light breeze carrying the fish odor of Fustian dwellings across the broad cobbled avenue. A few mature Fustians lumbered heavily along in the shade of the low buildings, audibly wheezing under the burden of their immense carapaces. Among them, shell-less youths trotted briskly on scaly stub legs. The driver of the flat-car, a labor-caste Fustian with his guild colors emblazoned on his back, heaved at the tiller, swung the unwieldy conveyance through the shipyard gates, and creaked to a halt.

"Thus I come to the shipyard with frightful speed," he said in Fustian. "Well I know the way of the naked-backs, who move always in haste."

Retief, climbing down, handed him a coin. "You should take up professional racing," he said. "Dare-devil."

Retief crossed the littered yard and tapped at the door of a rambling shed. Boards creaked inside, then the door swung back. A gnarled ancient with tarnished facial scales and a weathered carapace peered out at Retief.

"Long may you sleep," Retief said. "I'd like to take a look around, if you don't mind. I understand you're laying the bed-plate for your new liner today."

"May you dream of the deeps," the old fellow mumbled. He waved a stumpy arm toward a group of shell-less Fustians standing by a massive hoist. "The youths know more of bed-plates than do I, who but tend the place of papers."

"I know how you feel, old-timer," Retief said. "That sounds like the story of my life. Among your papers do you have a set of plans for the vessel? I understand it's to be a passenger liner."

The oldster nodded. He shuffled to a drawing file, rummaged, pulled out a sheaf of curled prints, and spread them on the table. Retief stood silently, running a finger over the uppermost drawing, tracing lines...

"What does the naked-back here?" a deep voice barked behind Retief. He turned. A heavy-faced Fustian youth, wrapped in a mantle, stood at the open door. Beady yellow eyes set among fine scales bored into Retief.

"I came to take a look at your new liner," said Retief.

"We need no prying foreigners here," the youth snapped. His eye fell on the drawings; he hissed in anger.

"Doddering hulk!" he snapped at the ancient, moving toward them. "May you toss in nightmares! Put aside the plans!"

"My mistake," Retief said. "I didn't know this was a secret project."

The youth hesitated. "It is not a secret," he muttered. "Why should it be a secret?"

"You tell me."

The youth worked his jaws and rocked his head from side to side in the Fustian gesture of uncertainty. "There is nothing to conceal," he said. "We merely construct a passenger liner."

"Then you don't mind if I look over the drawings," Retief said. "Who knows, maybe some day I'll want to reserve a suite for the trip out."

The youth turned and disappeared. Retief grinned at the oldster. "Went for his big brother, I guess," he said. "I have a feeling I won't get to study these in peace here. Mind if I copy them?"

"Willingly, light-footed one," said the old Fustian. "And mine is the shame for the discourtesy of youth."

Retief took out a tiny camera, flipped a copying lens in place, leafed through the drawings, clicking the shutter.

"A plague on these youths," said the oldster. "They grow more virulent day by day."

"Why don't you elders clamp down?"

"Agile are they and we are slow of foot. And this unrest is new; unknown in my youth was such insolence."

"The police—"

"Bah," the ancient rumbled. "None have we worthy of the name, nor have we needed them before now."

"What's behind it?"

"They have found leaders. The spiv, Slock, is one. And I fear they plot mischief." He pointed to the window. "They come, and a soft-one with them."

Retief, pocketing the camera, glanced out the window. A pale-featured Groacian with an ornately decorated crest stood with the youths, who eyed the hut, then started toward it.

"That's the military attaché of the Groaci Embassy," Retief said. "I wonder what he and the boys are cooking up together?"

"Naught that augurs well for the dignity of Fust," the oldster rumbled. "Flee, agile one, while I engage their attentions."

"I was just leaving," Retief said. "Which way out?"

"The rear door," the Fustian gestured with a stubby member. "Rest well, stranger on these shores," he said, moving to the entrance.

"Same to you, pop," said Retief. "And thanks."

He eased through the narrow back entrance, waited until voices were raised at the front of the shed, then strolled off toward the gate.

It was an hour along in the second dark of the third cycle when Retief left the Embassy technical library and crossed the corridor to his office. He flipped on a light and found a note tucked under a paperweight:

"Retief: I shall expect your attendance at the IAS dinner at first dark of the fourth cycle. There will be a brief but, I hope, impressive sponsorship ceremony for the SCARS group, with full press coverage, arrangements for which I have managed to complete in spite of your intransigence."

Retief snorted and glanced at his watch: less than three hours. Just time to creep home by flat-car, dress in ceremonial uniform, and creep back.

Outside he flagged a lumbering bus, stationed himself in a corner of it, and watched the yellow sun, Beta, rise above the low skyline. The nearby sea was at high tide now, under the pull of the major sun and the three moons, and the stiff breeze carried a mist of salt spray. Retief turned up his collar against the dampness. In half an hour he would be perspiring under the vertical rays of a first-noon sun, but the thought failed to keep the chill off.

Two youths clambered up on the moving platform and walked purposefully toward Retief. He moved off the rail, watching them, his weight balanced.

"That's close enough, kids," he said. "Plenty of room on this scow; no need to crowd up."

"There are certain films," the lead Fustian muttered. His voice was unusually deep for a Youth. He was wrapped in a heavy cloak and moved awkwardly. His adolescence was nearly at an end, Retief guessed.

"I told you once," Retief said. "Don't crowd me."

The two stepped close, their slit mouths snapping in anger. Retief put out a foot, hooked it behind the scaly leg of the over-age juvenile, and threw his weight against the cloaked chest. The clumsy Fustian tottered, then fell heavily. Retief was past him and off the flat-car before the other youth had completed his vain lunge toward the spot Retief had occupied. The Terrestrial waved cheerfully at the pair, hopped aboard another vehicle, and watched his would-be assailants lumber down off their car and move heavily off, their tiny heads twisted to follow his retreating figure.

So they wanted the film? Retief reflected, thumbing a cigar alight. They were a little late. He had already filed it in the Embassy vault, after running a copy for the reference files. And a comparison of the drawings with those of the obsolete Mark XXXV battle cruiser used two hundred years earlier by the Concordiat Naval Arm showed them to be almost identical-gun emplacements and all. And the term obsolete was a relative one. A ship, which had been outmoded in the armories of the Galactic Powers, could still be king of the walk in the Eastern Arm.

But how had these two known of the film? There had been no one present but himself and the old-timer—and Retief was willing to bet the elderly Fustian hadn't told them anything.

At least not willingly...

Retief frowned, dropped the cigar over the side, waited until the flat-car negotiated a mud-wallow, then swung down and headed for the shipyard.

The door, hinges torn loose, had been propped loosely back in position. Retief looked around at the battered interior of the shed. The old fellow had put up a struggle.

There were deep drag-marks in the dust behind the building. Retief followed them across the yard. They disappeared under the steel door of a warehouse.

Retief glanced around. Now, at the mid-hour of the fourth cycle, the workmen were heaped along the edge of the refreshment pond, deep in their siesta. Taking a multi-bladed tool from his pocket, Retief tried various fittings in the lock; it snicked open and he eased the door aside far enough to enter.

Heaped bales loomed before him. Snapping on the tiny lamp in the handle of the combination tool, Retief looked over the pile. One stack seemed out of alignment—and the dust had been scraped from the floor before it. He pocketed the light, climbed up on the bales, and looked over into a ring of bundles. The aged Fustian lay inside the ring, a heavy sack tied over his head. Retief dropped down beside him, sawed at the tough twine, and pulled the sack free.

"It's me, old fellow," he said, "the nosy stranger. Sorry I got you into this."

The oldster threshed his gnarled legs, rocked slightly, then fell back. "A curse on the cradle that rocked their infant slumbers," he rumbled. "But place me back on my feet and I hunt down the youth Slack though he flee to the bottommost muck of the Sea of Torments."

"How am I going to get you out of here? Maybe I'd better get some help."

"Nay. The perfidious youths abound here," said the old Fustian. "It would be your life."

"I doubt if they'd go that far."

"Would they not?" The Fustian stretched his neck. "Cast your light here. But for the toughness of my hide…"

Retief put the beam of the light on the leathery neck. A great smear of thick purplish blood welled from a ragged cut. The oldster chuckled: a sound like a seal coughing.

"Traitor they called me. For long they sawed at me—in vain. Then they trussed me and dumped me here. They think to return with weapons to complete the task."

"Weapons? I thought it was illegal—"

"Their evil genius, the Soft One," the Fustian said, "he would provide fuel to the Fire-Devil."

"The Groaci again," Retief said. "I wonder what their angle is."

"And I must confess: I told them of you, ere I knew their full intentions. Much can I tell you of their doings. But first, I pray: the block and tackle."

Retief found the hoist where the Fustian directed him, maneuvered it into position, hooked onto the edge of the carapace, and hauled away. The immense Fustian rose slowly, teetered...then flopped on his chest. Slowly he got to his feet.

"My name is Whonk, fleet one," he said. "My cows are yours."

"Thanks. I'm Retief. I'd like to meet the girls some time. But right now, let's get out of here."

Whonk leaned his bulk against the ponderous stacks of baled kelp, bull-dozing them aside. "Slow am I to anger," he said, "but implacable in my wrath. Slock, beware..."

"Hold it," said Retief suddenly. He sniffed. "What's that odor?" He flashed the light around, playing it over a dry stain on the floor. He knelt and sniffed at the spot.

"What kind of cargo was stacked here, Whonk? And where is it now?"

Whonk considered. "There were drums," he said. "Four of them, quite small, painted an evil green—the property of the Soft Ones, the Groaci. They lay here a day and a night. At full dark of the first period they came with stevedores and loaded them aboard the barge *Moss Rock*."

"The VIP boat. Who's scheduled to use it?"

"I know not. But what matters this? Let us discuss cargo movements after I have settled a score with certain youths."

"We'd better follow this up first, Whonk. There's only one substance I know of that's transported in drums and smells like that blot on the floor. That's titanite: the hottest explosive this side of a uranium pile."

Beta was setting as Retief, with Whonk puffing at his heels, came up to the sentry box beside the gangway leading to the plush interior of the Official Barge *Moss Rock*.

"A sign of the times," Whonk said, glancing inside the empty shelter. "A guard should stand here, but I see him not. Doubtless he crept away to sleep."

"Let's go aboard, and take a look around."

They entered the ship. Soft lights glowed in utter silence. A rough box stood on the floor, rollers and pry-bars beside it—a discordant note in the muted luxury of the setting. Whonk rummaged through its contents.

"Curious," he said. "What means this?" He held up a stained Fustian cloak of orange and green, a metal bracelet, and a stack of papers.

"Orange and green," Retief muttered. "Whose colors are those?"

"I know not..." Whonk glanced at the arm-band. "But this is lettered." He passed the metal band to Retief.

"SCARS," Retief read. He looked at Whonk. "It seems to me I've heard the name before," he murmured. "Let's get back to the Embassy—fast."

Back on the ramp Retief heard a sound...and turned in time to duck the charge of a hulking Fustian youth who thundered past him, and fetched up against the broad chest of Whonk, who locked him in a warm embrace.

"Nice catch, Whonk. Where'd he sneak out of?"

"The lout hid there by the storage bin," Whonk rumbled. The captive youth thumped his fists and toes futilely against the oldster's carapace.

"Hang on to him," Retief said. "He looks like the biting kind."

"No fear. Clumsy I am, yet I am not without strength."

"Ask him where the titanite is tucked away."

"Speak, witless grub," Whonk growled, "lest I tweak you in two."

The youth gurgled.

"Better let up before you make a mess of him," Retief said. Whonk lifted the youth clear of the floor, then flung him down with a thump that made the ground quiver. The younger Fustian glared up at the elder, his mouth snapping.

"This one was among those who trussed me and hid me away for the killing," said Whonk. "In his repentance he will tell all to his elder."

"He's the same one that tried to strike up an acquaintance with me on the bus," Retief said. "He gets around."

The youth, scrambling to his hands and knees, scuttled for freedom. Retief planted a foot on the dragging cloak; it ripped free. He stared at the bare back of the Fustian.

"By the Great Egg!" Whonk exclaimed, tripping the captive as he tried to rise. "This is no youth! His carapace has been taken from him."

Retief looked at the scarred back. "I thought he looked a little old. But I thought—"

"This is not possible," Whonk said wonderingly. "The great nerve trunks are deeply involved; not even the cleverest surgeon could excise the carapace and leave the patient living."

"It looks like somebody did the trick. But let's take this boy with us and get out of here. His folks may come home."

"Too late," said Whonk. Retief turned. Three youths came from behind the sheds.

"Well," Retief said. "It looks like the SCARS are out in force tonight. Where's your pal?" he said to the advancing trio, "the sticky little bird with the eye-stalks? Back at his Embassy, leaving you suckers holding the bag, I'll bet."

"Shelter behind me, Retief," said Whonk.

"Go get 'em, old-timer." Retief stooped and picked up one of the pry-bars. "I'll jump around and distract them."

Whonk let out a whistling roar and charged for the immature Fustians. They fanned out...one tripped, sprawling on his face. Retief, whirling the metal bar that he had thrust between the Fustian's legs, slammed it against the skull of another, who shook his head, then turned on Retief...and bounced off the steel hull of the *Moss Rock* as Whonk took him in full charge.

Retief used the bar on another head; his third blow laid the Fustian on the pavement, oozing purple. The other two club members departed hastily, dented but still mobile.

Retief leaned on his club, breathing hard. "Tough heads these kids have got. I'm tempted to chase those two lads down, but I've got another errand to run. I don't know who the Groaci intended to blast, but I have a suspicion somebody of importance was scheduled for a boat ride in the next few hours, and three drums of titanite is enough to vaporize this tub and everyone aboard her."

"The plot is foiled," said Whonk. "But what reason did they have?"

"The Groaci are behind it. I have an idea the SCARS didn't know about this gambit."

"Which of these is the leader?" asked Whonk. He prodded a fallen youth. "Arise, dreaming one."

"Never mind him, Whonk. We'll tie these two up and leave them here. I know where to find the boss."

A stolid-looking crowd fined the low-ceilinged banquet hall. Retief scanned the tables for the pale blobs of Terrestrial faces, dwarfed by the giant armored bodies of the

Fustians. Across the room Magnan fluttered a hand. Retief headed toward him. A low-pitched vibration filled the air, the rumble of sub-sonic Fustian music.

Retief slid into his place beside Magnan. "Sorry to be late, Mr. Ambassador."

"I'm honored that you chose to appear at all," Magnan said coldly. He turned back to the Fustian on his left.

"Ah, yes, Mr. Minister," he said. "Charming, most charming. So joyous."

The Fustian looked at him, beady-eyed. "It is the Lament of Hatching," he said, "our National Dirge."

"Oh," said Magnan. "how interesting. Such a pleasing balance of instruments."

"It is a droon solo," said the Fustian, eyeing the Terrestrial Ambassador suspiciously.

"Why don't you just admit you can't hear it," Retief whispered loudly. "And if I may interrupt a moment—"

Magnan cleared his throat. "Now that our Mr. Retief has arrived, perhaps we could rush right along to the sponsorship ceremonies…"

"This group," said Retief, leaning across Magnan to speak to the Fustian, "the SCARS…how much do you know about them, Mr. Minister?"

"Nothing at all," the huge Fustian elder rumbled. "For my taste, all youths should be kept penned with the livestock until they grow a carapace to tame their irresponsibility."

"We mustn't lose sight of the importance of channeling youthful energies," said Magnan.

"Labor gangs," said the minister. "In my youth we were indentured to the dredge-masters. I myself drew a muck-sledge."

"But in these modem times," put in Retief, "surely it's incumbent on us to make happy these golden hours."

The minister snorted. "Last week I had a golden hour: they set upon me and pelted me with over-ripe dung-fruit."

"But this was merely a manifestation of normal youthful frustrations," cried Magnan. "Their essential tenderness—"

"You'd not find a tender spot on that lout yonder," the minister said, pointing with a fork at a newly arrived youth, if you drilled bore holes and blasted. "

"Why, that's our guest of honor," said Magnan, "a fine young fellow, Slop I believe his name is—"

"Slock," said Retief. "Nine feet of armor-plated orneriness. And—"

Magnan rose, tapping on his glass. The Fustians winced at the, to them, supersonic vibrations, and looked at each other muttering. Magnan tapped louder. The minister drew in his head, his eyes closed. Some of the Fustians rose and tottered for the doors; the noise level rose. Magnan redoubled his efforts. The glass broke with a clatter, and green wine gushed on the tablecloth.

"What in the name of the Great Egg." the minister muttered. He blinked, breathing deeply.

"Oh, forgive me," Magnan blurted, dabbing at the wine.

"Too bad the glass gave out," Retief said. "In another minute you'd have cleared the hall—and then maybe I could have gotten a word in. You see, Mr. Minister," he said, turning to the Fustian, "there is a matter you should know about…"

"Your attention, please," Magnan said, rising. "I see that our fine young guest of honor has arrived, and I hope that the remainder of his committee will be along in a moment. It is my pleasure to announce that our Mr. Retief has had the good fortune to win out in the keen bidding for the pleasure of sponsoring this lovely group, and—"

Retief tugged at Magnan's sleeve. "Don't introduce me yet," he said. "I want to appear suddenly—more dramatic, you know."

"Well," Magnan murmured, glancing down at Retief, "I'm gratified to see you entering into the spirit of the event at last." He turned his attention back to the assembled guests. "If our honored guest will join me on the rostrum…" he said. "The gentlemen of the press may want to catch a few shots of the presentation."

Magnan moved from his place, made his way forward, stepped up on the low platform at the center of the wide room, took his place beside the robed Fustian youth, and beamed at the cameras.

"How gratifying it is to take this opportunity to express once more the great pleasure we have in sponsoring SCARS," Magnan said, talking slowly for the benefit of the scribbling reporters. "We'd like to think that in our modest way we're to be a part of all that the SCARS achieve during the years ahead…"

Magnan paused as a huge Fustian elder heaved his bulk up the two low steps to the rostrum and approached the guest of honor. He watched as the newcomer paused behind Slock, who was busy returning the stares of the spectators and did not notice the new arrival.

Retief pushed through the crowd and stepped up to face the Fustian youth. Slock stared at him, drawing back.

"You know me, Slock," Retief said loudly. "An old fellow named Whonk told you about me, just before you tried to saw off his head, remember? It was when I came out to take a look at that battle cruiser you're building."

With a bellow Slock reached for Retief—and choked off in mid-cry as Whonk pinioned him from behind, lifting the youth clear of the floor.

"Glad you reporters happened along," Retief said to the gaping newsmen. "Slack here had a deal with a sharp operator from the Groaci Embassy. The Groaci were to supply the necessary hardware and Slack, as foreman at the shipyards, was to see that everything was properly installed. The next step, I assume, would have been a local take-over, followed by a little interplanetary war on Flamenco or one of the other nearby worlds...for which the Groaci would be glad to supply plenty of ammo."

Magnan found his tongue. "Are you mad, Retief?" he screeched. "This group was vouched for by the Ministry of Youth."

"That Ministry's overdue for a purge," Retief said. He turned back to Slock. "I wonder if you were in on the little diversion that was planned for today. When the *Moss Rock* blew, a variety of clues were to be planted where they'd be easy to find...with SCARS written all over them. The Groaci would thus have neatly laid the whole affair squarely at the door of the Terrestrial Embassy...whose sponsorship of the SCARS had received plenty of publicity."

"The *Moss Rock?*" Magnan said. "But that was—Retief! This is idiotic. The SCARS themselves were scheduled to go on a cruise tomorrow."

Slock roared suddenly, twisting violently. Whonk teetered, his grip loosened...and Slock pulled free and was off the platform, butting his way through the milling oldsters on the dining room floor. Magnan watched, openmouthed.

"The Groaci were playing a double game, as usual," Retief said. "They intended to dispose of these lads after they got things under way."

"Well, don't stand there," Magnan yelped. "Do something! If Slop is the ringleader of a delinquent gang—" He moved to give chase himself.

Retief grabbed his arm. "Don't jump down there," he called above the babble of talk. "You'd have as much chance of getting through there as a jack rabbit through a threshing contest. Where's a phone?"

Ten minutes later the crowd had thinned slightly. "We can get through now," Whonk called. "This way." He lowered himself to the floor and bulled through to the exit. Flash bulbs popped. Retief and Magnan followed in Honk's wake.

In the lounge Retief grabbed the phone, waited for the operator, and gave a code letter. No reply. He tried another.

"No good," he said after a full minute had passed. He slammed the phone back in its niche. "Let's grab a cab."

In the street the blue sun, Alpha, peered like an arc light under a low cloud layer. Flat shadows lay across the mud of the avenue. The three mounted a passing flat-car. Whonk squatted, resting the weight of his immense shell on the heavy plank flooring.

"Would that I, too, could lose this burden, as has the false youth we bludgeoned aboard the *Moss Rock*," he sighed. "Soon will I be forced into retirement; and a mere keeper of a place of papers such as I will rate no more than a slab on the public strand, with once-daily feedings. Even for a man of high position retirement is no pleasure. A slab in the Park of Monuments is little better. A dismal outlook for one's next thousand years."

"You two continue on to the police station," Retief said. "I want to play a hunch. But don't take too long. I may be painfully right."

"What—?" Magnan started.

"As you wish, Retief," Whonk said.

The flat-car trundled past the gate to the shipyard and Retief jumped down and headed at a run for the VIP boat.

The guard post still stood vacant. The two youths that he and Whonk had left trussed were gone.

"That's the trouble with a peaceful world," Retief muttered. "No police protection." Stepping down from the lighted entry, he took up a position behind the sentry box. Alpha rose higher, shedding a glaring white light without heat. Retief shivered.

There was a sound in the near entrance, like two elephants colliding. Retief looked toward the gate. His giant acquaintance, Whonk, had reappeared and was grappling with a hardly less massive opponent. A small figure became visible in the melee, scuttled for the gate, was headed off by the battling titans, turned and made for the opposite side of the shipyard. Retief waited, jumped out and gathered in the fleeing Groacian.

"Well, Yith," he said, "how's tricks…? you should pardon the expression."

"Release me, Retief!" the pale-featured creature lisped, his throat bladder pulsating in agitation. "The behemoths vie for the privilege of dismembering me."

"I know how they feel. I'll see what I can do…for a price."

"I appeal to you," Yith whispered hoarsely, "as a fellow diplomat, a fellow alien, a fellow soft-back."

"Why don't you appeal to Slock, as a fellow conspirator?" Retief said. "Now keep quiet…and you may get out of this alive."

The heavier of the two struggling Fustians threw the other to the ground. The smaller Fustian lay on its back, helpless.

"That's Whonk, still on his feet," Retief said. "I wonder who he's caught—and why."

Whonk came toward the *Moss Rock* dragging the supine Fustian. Retief thrust Yith down well out of sight behind the sentry box. "Better sit tight, Yith. Don't try to sneak off; I

can outrun you. Stay here and I'll see what I can do."
Stepping out, he hailed Whonk.

Puffing like a steam engine, Whonk pulled up before him.
"Hail, Retief!" he panted. "You followed a hunch; I did the
same. I saw something strange in this one when we passed
him on the avenue. I watched, followed him here. Look! It
is Slock, strapped into a dead carapace! Now many things
become clear."

Retief whistled. "So the youths aren't all as young as they
look. Somebody's been holding out on the rest of you
Fustians."

"The soft one," Whonk said. "You laid him by the heels,
Retief. I saw. Produce him now."

"Hold on a minute, Whonk. It won't do you any good
to—"

Whonk winked broadly. "I must take my revenge!" he
roared. "I shall test the texture of the Soft One! His pulped
remains will be scoured up by the ramp-washers and mailed
home in bottles."

Retief whirled at a sound, caught up with the scuttling
Yith fifty feet away, and hauled him back to Whonk.

"It's up to you, Whonk," he said. "I know how important
ceremonial revenge is to you Fustians."

"Mercy!" Yith hissed, his eye-stalks whipping in distress.
"I claim diplomatic immunity."

"No diplomat am I," Whonk rumbled. "Let me see;
suppose I start with one of those obscenely active eyes." He
reached...

"I have an idea," Retief said brightly. "Do you suppose—
just this once—you could forego the ceremonial revenge if
Yith promised to arrange for a Groacian Surgical Mission to
de-carapace you elders?"

"But," Whonk protested, "those eyes; what a pleasure to
pluck them, one by one—"

153

"Yess," Yith hissed, "I swear it; our most expert surgeons…platoons of them, with the finest of equipment."

"I have dreamed of how it would be to sit on this one, to feel him squash beneath my bulk…"

"Light as a whissle feather shall you dance," Yith whispered. "Shell-less shall you spring in the joy of renewed youth…"

"Maybe, just one eye," Whonk said. "That would leave him four…"

"Be a sport," said Retief.

"Well."

"It's a deal then," Retief said. "Yith, on your word as a diplomat, an alien, and a soft-back, you'll set up the mission. Groaci surgical skill is an export that will net you more than armaments. It will be a whissle feather in your cap—if you bring it off. And in return, Whonk won't sit on you. In addition, I won't prefer charges against you of interference in the internal affairs of a free world."

Behind Whonk there was a movement. Slock, wriggling free of the borrowed carapace, struggled to his feet in time for Whonk to seize him, lift him high, and head for the entry to the *Moss Rock*.

"Hey," Retief called. "Where are you going?"

"I would not deny this one his reward," Whonk called. "He hoped to cruise in luxury; so be it."

"Hold on," Retief said. "That tub is loaded with titanite!"

"Stand not in my way, Retief. For this one in truth owes me a vengeance."

Retief watched as the immense Fustian bore his giant burden up the ramp and disappeared within the ship.

"I guess Whonk means business," he said to Yith, who hung in his grasp, all five eyes goggling. "And he's a little too big for me to stop, once he sets his mind on something. But maybe he's just throwing a scare into him."

Whonk reappeared, alone, and climbed down. "What did you do with him?" Retief said.

"We had best withdraw," Whonk said. "The killing radius of the drive is fifty yards."

"You mean—"

"The controls are set for Groac. Long may he sleep."

"It was quite a bang," Retief said, "but I guess you saw it too."

"No, confound it," Magnan said. "When I remonstrated with Hulk, or Whelk—"

"Whonk."

"—the ruffian thrust me into an alley, bound in my own cloak. I'll most certainly mention the indignity in a note to the Minister." He jotted on a pad.

"How about the surgical mission?"

"A most generous offer," Magnan said. "Frankly, I was astonished. I think perhaps we've judged the Groaci too harshly."

"I hear the Ministry of Youth has had a rough morning of it," Retief said. "And a lot of rumors are flying to the effect that Youth Groups are on the way out."

Magnan cleared his throat and shuffled papers. "I—ah—have explained to the press that last night's ahh…"

"Fiasco."

"—affair was necessary in order to place the culprits in an untenable position. Of course, as to the destruction of the VIP vessel and the presumed death of the fellow, Slop—"

"The Fustians understand," Retief said. "Whonk wasn't kidding about ceremonial vengeance. Yith was lucky: he hadn't actually drawn blood. Then no amount of dickering would have saved him."

"The Groaci have been guilty of gross misuse of diplomatic privilege," Magnan said. "I think that a note—or perhaps an *aide memoire:* less formal…"

"The *Moss Rock* was bound for Groac," Retief said. "She was already in her transit orbit when she blew. The major fragments should arrive on schedule in a month or so. It should provide quite a meteorite display. I think that should be all the aid the Groaci's *memoires* will need to keep their tentacles off Fust."

"But diplomatic usage—"

"Then, too, the less that's put in writing, the less they can blame you for, if anything goes wrong."

"There's that, of course," Magnan said, his lips pursed. "Now you're thinking constructively, Retief. We may make a diplomat of you yet." He smiled expansively.

"Maybe. But I refuse to let it depress me." Retief stood up. "I'm taking a few weeks off…if you have no objections, Mr. Ambassador. My pal Whonk wants to show me an island down south where the fishing is good."

"But there are some extremely important matters coming up," Magnan said. "We're planning to sponsor Senior Citizen Groups.

"Count me out. Groups give me an itch."

"Why, what an astonishing remark, Retief. After all, we diplomats are ourselves a group."

"Uh, huh," Retief said. "That's what I mean."

Magnan sat quietly, his mouth open, and watched as Retief stepped into the hall and closed the door gently behind him.

...No jackstraws to be swayed by superficial appearances, dedicated career field personnel of the Corps unflaggingly administered the enlightened concepts evolved at Corps HQ by high-level deep-think teams toiling unceasingly in underground caverns to weld the spirit of Inter-Being amity. Never has the efficacy of close cultural rapport, coupled with Mission teamwork, been better displayed than in the loyal performance of Administrative Assistant Yolanda Meuhl, Acting Consul at Groac, in maintaining the Corps posture laid down by her predecessor, Consul Whaffle...
Vol VII, reel 98. 488 A. E. (AD 2949)

POLICY

"THE CONSUL for the Terrestrial States," Retief said, "presents his compliments, et cetera, to the Ministry of Culture of the Groacian Autonomy, and, with reference to the Ministry's invitation to attend a recital of interpretive grimacing, has the honor to express regret that he will be unable—"

"You can't turn down this invitation," Administrative Assistant Meuhl said flatly. "I'll make that accepts with pleasure.

Retief exhaled a plume of cigar smoke.

"Miss Meuhl," he said, "in the past couple of weeks I've sat through six light concerts, four attempts at chamber music, and God knows how many assorted folk-art festivals. I've been tied up every off-duty hour since I got here."

"You can't offend the Groaci," Miss Meuhl said sharply. "Consul Whaffle would never have—"

"Whaffle left here three months ago," Retief said, "leaving me in charge."

"Well," Miss Meuhl said, snapping off the dictyper. "I'm sure I don't know what excuse I can give the Minister."

"Never mind the excuses. Just tell him I won't be there." He stood up.

"Are you leaving the office?" Miss Meuhl adjusted her glasses. "I have some important letters here for your signature."

"I don't recall dictating any letters today, Miss Meuhl," Retief said, pulling on a light cape.

"I wrote them for you. They're just as Consul Whaffle would have wanted them."

"Did you write all Whaffle's letters for him, Miss Meuhl?"

"Consul Whaffle was an extremely busy man," Miss Meuhl said stiffly. "He had complete confidence in me."

"Since I'm cutting out the culture from now on, I won't be so busy."

"Well! May I ask where you'll be if something comes up?"

"I'm going over to the Foreign Office Archives."

Miss Meuhl blinked behind thick lenses. "Whatever for?"

Retief looked at her thoughtfully. "You've been here on Groac for four years, Miss Meuhl. What was behind the coup d'etat that put the present government in power?"

"I'm sure I haven't pried into—"

"What about that Terrestrial cruiser, the one that disappeared out this way about ten years back?"

"Mr. Retief, those are just the sort of questions we avoid with the Groaci. I certainly hope you're not thinking of openly intruding—"

"Why?"

"The Groaci are a very sensitive race. They don't welcome outworlders raking up things. They've been gracious enough to let us live down the fact that Terrestrials subjected them to deep humiliation on one occasion."

"You mean when we came looking for the cruiser?"

"I, for one, am ashamed of the high-handed tactics that were employed, grilling these innocent people as though they were criminals. We try never to reopen that wound, Mr. Retief."

"They never found the cruiser, did they?"

"Certainly not on Groac."

Retief nodded. "Thanks, Miss Meuhl," he said. "I'll be back before you close the office." Miss Meuhl's thin face was set in lines of grim disapproval as he closed the door.

Peering through the small grilled window, the pale-featured Groacian vibrated his throat-bladder in a distressed bleat.

"Not to enter the Archives," he said in his faint voice. "The denial of permission. The deep regret of the Archivist."

"The importance of my task here," Retief said, enunciating the glottal language with difficulty. "My interest in local history."

"The impossibility of access to outworlders. To depart quietly."

"The necessity that I enter."

"The specific instructions of the Archivist." The Groacian's voice rose to a whisper. "To insist no longer. To give up this idea!"

"Okay, skinny, I know when I'm licked," Retief said in Terran. "To keep your nose clean."

Outside, Retief stood for a moment looking across at the deeply carved windowless stucco facades lining the street, then started off in the direction of the Terrestrial Consulate General. The few Groacians on the street eyed him furtively, and veered to avoid him as he passed. Flimsy high-wheeled ground cars puffed silently along the resilient pavement. The air was clean and cool. At the office Miss Meuhl would be waiting with another list of complaints. Retief studied the carving over the open doorways along the street. An elaborate one picked out in pinkish paint seemed to indicate the Groacian equivalent of a bar. Retief went in.

A Groacian bartender dispensing clay pots of alcoholic drink from the bar-pit at the center of the room looked at Retief, then froze in mid-motion, a metal tube poised over a waiting pot.

"A cooling drink," Retief said in Groacian, squatting down at the edge of the pit. "To sample a true Groacian beverage."

"Not to enjoy my poor offerings," the Groacian mumbled. "A pain in the digestive sacs. To express regret."

"Not to worry," Retief replied. "To pour it out and let me decide whether I like it."

"To be grappled in by peace-keepers for poisoning of...foreigners." The barkeep looked around for support, but found none. The Groaci customers, eyes elsewhere, were drifting out.

"To get the lead out," Retief said, placing a thick gold-piece in the dish provided. "To shake a tentacle."

"To procure a cage," a thin voice called from the sidelines. "To display the freak."

Retief turned. A tall Groacian vibrated his mandibles in a gesture of contempt. From his bluish throat coloration it was apparent the creature was drunk.

"To choke in your upper sac," the bartender hissed, extending his eyes toward the drunk. "To keep silent, littermate of drones."

"To swallow your own poison, dispenser of vileness," the drunk whispered. "To find a proper cage for this zoo-piece." He wavered toward Retief. "To show this one in the streets, like all freaks."

"Seen a lot of freaks like me, have you?" Retief asked interestedly.

"To speak intelligibly, malodorous outworlder," the drunk said. The barkeep whispered something and two customers came up to the drunk, took his arms, and helped him to the door.

"To get a cage," the drunk shrilled. "To keep the animals in their place…"

"I've changed my mind," Retief said to the bartender. "To be grateful as hell, but to have to hurry off now." He followed the drunk out the door. The other Groaci, releasing the heckler, hurried back inside. Retief looked at the weaving creature.

"To begone, freak," the Groacian whispered.

"To be pals," Retief said. "To be kind to dumb animals."

"To have you hauled away to a stockyard; ill-odored foreign livestock."

"Not to be angry, fragrant native," Retief said. "To permit me to chum with you."

"To flee before I take a cane to you!"

"To have a drink together."

"Not to endure such insolence." The Groacian advanced toward Retief. Retief backed away.

"To hold hands," he said. "To be buddies—"

The Groacian reached for him, but missed. A passer-by stepped around him, head down, and scuttled away. Retief, backing into the opening to a narrow cross-way, offered further verbal familiarities to the drunken local, who followed, furious. Retief stepped around him, seized his collar and yanked. The Groacian fell on his back. Retief stood over him. The downed native half rose; Retief put a foot against his chest and pushed.

"Not to be going anywhere for a few minutes," he said. "To stay right here and have a nice long talk."

"There you are!" Miss Meuhl said, eyeing Retief over her lenses. "There are two gentlemen waiting to see you. Groacian gentlemen."

"Government men, I imagine. Word travels fast." Retief pulled off his cape. "This saves me the trouble of paying another call at the Foreign Ministry."

"What have you been doing? They seem very upset, I don't mind telling you."

"I'm sure you don't. Come along—and bring an official recorder.

Two Groaci, wearing heavy eye-shields and elaborate crest ornaments indicative of rank, rose as Retief entered the room. Neither offered a courteous snap of the mandibles, Retief noted; they were mad, all right.

"I am Fith, of the Terrestrial Desk, Ministry of Foreign Affairs," the taller Groacian said, in lisping Terran. "May I present Shluh, of the Internal Police."

"Sit down, gentlemen," Retief said. They resumed their seats. Miss Meuhl hovered nervously, then sat down on the edge of a chair.

"Oh, it's such a pleasure—" she began.

"Never mind that," Retief said. "These gentlemen didn't come here to sip tea today."

"True," Fith rasped. "Frankly, I have had a most disturbing report, Mr. Consul. I shall ask Shluh to recount it." He nodded to the police chief.

"One hour ago," Shluh said, "a Groacian national was brought to hospital suffering from serious contusions. Questioning of this individual revealed that he had been set upon and beaten by a foreigner; a Terrestrial, to be precise. Investigation by my Department indicates that the description of the culprit closely matches that of the Terrestrial Consul..."

Miss Meuhl gasped audibly.

"Have you ever heard," Retief said, looking steadily at Fith, "of a Terrestrial cruiser, the *ISV Terrific*, which dropped from sight in this sector nine years ago?"

"Really!" Miss Meuhl exclaimed, rising, "I wash my hands—"

"Just keep that recorder going," Retief snapped.

"I'll not be a party—"

"You'll do as you're told, Miss Meuhl," Retief said quietly. "I'm telling you to make an official sealed record of this conversation."

Miss Meuhl sat down.

Fith puffed out his throat indignantly. "You re-open an old wound, Mr. Consul. It reminds us of certain illegal treatment at Terrestrial hands."

"Hogwash," Retief said. "That tune went over with my predecessors, but it hits a sour note with me."

"All our efforts," Miss Meuhl said, "to live down that terrible episode; and you—"

"Terrible? I understand that a Terrestrial Peace Enforcer stood off Groac and sent a delegation down to ask questions. They got some funny answers and stayed on to dig around a little. After a week, they left. Somewhat annoying to you Groaci, if you were innocent—"

"*If!*" Miss Meuhl burst out.

"If, indeed," Fith said, his weak voice trembling. "I must protest your—"

"Save your protests, Fith. You have some explaining to do, and I don't think your story will be good enough."

"It is for you to explain; this person who was beaten—"

"Not beaten; just rapped a few times to loosen his memory."

"Then you admit—"

"It worked, too. He remembered lots of things, once he put his mind to it."

Fith rose; Shluh followed suit.

"I shall ask for your immediate recall, Mr. Consul. Were it not for your diplomatic immunity, I should—"

"Why did the Government fall, Fith, just after the Task Force paid its visit, and before the arrival of the first Terrestrial diplomatic mission?"

"This is an internal matter," Fith cried, in his faint Groacian voice. "The new regime has shown itself most amiable to you Terrestrials; it has outdone itself—"

"—to keep the Terrestrial Consul and his staff in the dark," Retief said, "and the same goes for the few Terrestrial businessmen you've given visas. This continual round of culture; no social contacts outside the diplomatic circle; no travel permits to visit outlying districts or your satellite—"

"Enough!" Fith's mandibles quivered in distress. "I can talk no more of this matter."

"You'll talk to me, or there'll be a squadron of Peace Enforcers here in five days to do the talking," Retief said.

"You can't—" Miss Meuhl gasped.

Retief turned a steady look on Miss Meuhl. She closed her mouth. The Groaci sat down.

"Answer me this one," Retief said, looking at Shluh. "A few years back—nine, to be exact—there was a little parade held here. Some curious-looking creatures were captured, and after being securely caged, were exhibited to the gentle Groacian public. Hauled through the streets. Very educational, no doubt. A highly cultural show.

"Funny thing about these animals: they wore clothes, seemed to communicate with each other. Altogether a very; amusing exhibit.

"Tell me, Shluh, what happened to those six Terrestrials after the parade was over?"

Fith made a choked noise, then spoke rapidly to Shluh in Groacian. Shluh, retracting his eyes, shrank down in his chair. Miss Meuhl opened her mouth, then closed it.

"How did they die?" Retief snapped. "Did you cut their throats, shoot them, bury them alive? What amusing end did you figure out for them? Research, maybe. Cut them open to see what made them yell..."

"No," Fith gasped. "I must correct this terrible false impression at once."

"False impression, hell," Retief said. "They were Terrans; a simple narco-interrogation would get that out of any Groacian who saw the parade."

"Yes," Fith said weakly. "It is true, they were Terrestrials. But there was no killing—"

"They're alive?"

"Alas, no. They...died."

"I see," Retief said. "They died."

"We tried to keep them alive, of course; but we did not know what foods—"

"Didn't take the trouble to find out."

"They fell ill," Fith said. "One by one..."

"We'll deal with that question later," Retief said. "Right now, I want more information. Where did you get them? Where did you hide the ship? What happened to the rest of the crew? Did they 'fall ill' before the big parade?"

"There were no more! Absolutely, I assure you!"

"Killed in the crash landing?"

"No crash landing. The ship descended intact, east of the city. The...Terrestrials...were unharmed. Naturally, we feared them; they were strange to us. We had never before seen such beings."

"Stepped off the ship with guns blazing, did they?"

"Guns? No, no guns—"

"They raised their hands, didn't they, asked for help? You helped them; helped them to death."

"How could we know?" Fith moaned.

"How could you know a flotilla would show up in a few months looking for them, you mean? That was a shock, wasn't I? I'll bet you had a brisk time of it hiding the ship, and shutting everybody up. A close call, eh?"

"We were afraid," Shluh said. "We are a simple people. We feared the strange creatures from the alien craft. We did not kill them, but we felt it was as well that they...did not survive. Then, when the warships came, we realized our error, but we feared to speak. We purged our guilty leaders, concealed what had happened, and...offered our friendship. We invited the opening of diplomatic relations. We made a blunder, it is true, a great blunder. But we have tried to make amends..."

"Where is the ship?"

"The ship?"

"What did you do with it? It was too big to just walk off and forget. Where is it?"

The two Groacians exchanged looks.

"We wish to show our contrition," Fith said. "We will show you the ship."

"Miss Meuhl," Retief said. "If I don't come back in a reasonable length of time, transmit that recording to Sector Headquarters, sealed." He stood and looked at the Groaci.

"Let's go," he said.

Retief stooped under the heavy timbers shoring the entry to the cavern and peered into the gloom at the curving flank of the space-burned hull.

"Any lights in here?" he asked.

A Groacian threw a switch and a weak bluish glow sprang up. Retief walked along the raised wooden catwalk, studying the ship. Empty emplacements gaped below lenseless scanner eyes. Littered decking was visible within the half-open entry port. Near the bow the words *IVS Terrific B7 New Terra'* were lettered in bright chrome duralloy.

"How did you get it in here?" Retief asked.

"It was hauled here from the landing point, some nine miles distant," Fith said, his voice thinner than ever. "This is a natural crevasse; the vessel was lowered into it and roofed over."

"How did you shield it so the detectors didn't pick it up?"

"All here is high-grade iron-ore," Fith said, waving a member. "Great veins of almost pure metal."

"Let's go inside."

Shluh came forward with a hand-lamp. The party entered the ship. Retief clambered up a narrow companionway and glanced around the interior of the control compartment. Dust was thick on the deck, the stanchions where acceleration couches had been mounted, the empty instrument panels, the litter of sheared bolts, and on scraps of wire and paper. A thin frosting of rust dulled the exposed metal where cutting torches had sliced away heavy shielding. There was a faint odor of stale bedding.

"The cargo compartment—" Shluh began.

"I've seen enough," Retief said. Silently, the Groacians led the way back out through the tunnel and into the late afternoon sunshine. As they climbed the slope to the steam car, Fith came to Retief's side.

"Indeed I hope that this will be the end of this unfortunate affair," he said. "Now that all has been fully and honestly shown."

"You can skip all that," Retief said. "You're nine years late. The crew was still alive when the Task Force called, I imagine. You killed them—or let them die—rather than take the chance of admitting what you'd done."

"We were at fault," Fith said abjectly. "Now we wish only friendship."

"The *Terrific* was a heavy cruiser, about twenty thousand tons." Retief looked grimly at the slender Foreign Office official. "Where is she, Fith? I won't settle for a hundred-ton lifeboat."

Fith erected his eye stalks so violently that one eye-shield fell off.

"I know nothing of...of..." He stopped. His throat vibrated rapidly as he struggled for calm.

"My government can entertain no further accusations, Mr. Consul," he said at last. "I have been completely candid with you, I have overlooked your probing into matters not properly within your sphere of responsibility. My patience is at an end."

"Where is that ship?" Retief rapped out. "You never learn, do you? You're still convinced you can hide the whole thing and forget it. I'm telling you you can't."

"We return to the city now," Fith said. "I can do no more."

"You can and you will, Fith," Retief said. "I intend to get to the truth of this matter."

Fith spoke to Shluh in rapid Groacian. The police chief gestured to his four armed constables. They moved to ring Retief in.

Retief eyed Fith. "Don't try it," he said. "You'll just get yourself in deeper."

Fith clacked his mandibles angrily, his eye stalks canted aggressively toward the Terrestrial.

"Out of deference to your diplomatic status, Terrestrial, I shall ignore your insulting implications," Fith said in his reedy voice. "We will now return to the city."

Retief looked at the four policemen. "Sure," he said. "We'll cover the details later."

Fith followed him into the car and sat rigidly at the far end of the seat.

"I advise you to remain very close to your Consulate," Fith said. "I advise you to dismiss these fancies from your mind, and to enjoy the cultural aspects of life at Groac. Especially, I should not venture out of the city, or appear overly curious about matters of concern only to the Groacian government."

In the front seat, Shluh looked straight ahead. The loosely-sprung vehicle bobbed and swayed along the narrow highway. Retief listened to the rhythmic puffing of the motor and said nothing.

"Miss Meuhl," Retief said, "I want you to listen carefully to what I'm going to tell you. I have to move rapidly now, to catch the Groaci off guard."

"I'm sure I don't know what you're talking about," Miss Meuhl snapped, her eyes sharp behind the heavy lenses.

"If you'll listen, you may find out," Retief said. "I have no time to waste, Miss Meuhl. They won't be expecting an immediate move—I hope—and that may give me the latitude I need."

"You're still determined to make an issue of that incident." Miss Meuhl snorted. "I really can hardly blame the Groaci; they are not a sophisticated race; they had never before met aliens."

"You're ready to forgive a great deal, Miss Meuhl. But it's not what happened nine years ago I'm concerned with. It's what's happening now. I've told you that it was only a lifeboat the Groaci have hidden out. Don't you understand the implication? That vessel couldn't have come far; the cruiser itself must be somewhere nearby. I want to know where."

"The Groaci don't know. They're a very cultured, gentle people. You can do irreparable harm to the Terrestrial image if you insist—"

"We're wasting time," Retief said, as he crossed the room to his desk, opened a drawer, and took out a slim-barreled needler.

"This office is being watched; not very efficiently, if I know the Groaci. I think I can get past them all right."

"Where are you going with…that?" Miss Meuhl stared at the needler. "What in the world—"

"The Groaci won't waste any time destroying every piece of paper in their files relating to this affair. I have to get what I need before it's too late. If I wait for an official Enquiry Commission, they'll find nothing but blank smiles."

"You're out of your mind!" Miss Meuhl stood up, quivering with indignation. "You're like a…a…"

"You and I are in a tight spot, Miss Meuhl. The logical next move for the Groaci is to dispose of both of us. We're the only ones who know what happened. Fith almost did the job this afternoon, but I bluffed him out—for the moment."

Miss Meuhl emitted a shrill laugh. "Your fantasies are getting the better of you," she gasped. "In danger, indeed! Disposing of me! I've never heard anything so ridiculous."

"Stay in this office. Close and safe-lock the door. You've got food and water in the dispenser. I suggest you stock up, before they shut the supply down. Don't let anyone in, on any pretext whatever. I'll keep in touch with you via handphone."

"What are you planning to do?"

"If I don't make it back here, transmit the sealed record of this afternoon's conversation, along with the information I've given you. Beam it through on a Mayday priority. Then tell the Groaci what you've done and sit tight. I think you'll be all right. It won't be easy to blast in here and anyway, they won't make things worse by killing you in an obvious way. A Force can be here in a week."

"I'll do nothing of the sort! The Groaci are very fond of me! You...Johnny-come-lately! Roughneck! Setting out to destroy—"

"Blame it on me if it will make you feel any better," Retief said, "but don't be fool enough to trust them." He pulled on a cape and opened the door.

"I'll be back in a couple of hours," he said. Miss Meuhl stared after him silently as he closed the door.

It was an hour before dawn when Retief keyed the combination to the safe-lock and stepped into the darkened Consular office. Miss Meuhl, dozing in a chair, awoke with a start. She looked at Retief, rose, snapped on a light, and turned to stare.

"What in the world— Where have you been? What's happened to your clothing?"

"I got a little dirty—don't worry about it." Retief went to his desk, opened a drawer, and replaced the needler.

"Where have you been?" Miss Meuhl demanded. "I stayed here."

"I'm glad you did," Retief said. "I hope you piled up a supply of food and water from the dispenser, too. We'll be holed up here for a week, at least." He jotted figures on a pad. "Warm up the official sender. I have a long transmission for Sector Headquarters."

"Are you going to tell me where you've been?"

"I have a message to get off first, Miss Meuhl," Retief said sharply. "I've been to the Foreign Ministry," he added. "I'll tell you all about it later."

"At this hour? There's no one there."

"Exactly."

Miss Meuhl gasped. "You mean you broke in? You burgled the Foreign Office?"

"That's right," Retief said calmly. "Now—"

"This is absolutely the end," Miss Meuhl said. "Thank heaven I've already—"

"Get that sender going, woman! This is important."

"I've already done so, Mr. Retief!" Miss Meuhl said harshly.

"I've been waiting for you to come back here." She turned to the communicator and flipped levers. The screen snapped aglow, and a wavering long-distance image appeared.

"He's here now," Miss Meuhl said to the screen. She looked at Retief triumphantly.

"That's good," said Retief. "I don't think the Groaci can knock us off the air, but—"

"I have done my duty, Mr. Retief; I made a full report of your activities to Sector Headquarters last night, as soon as you left this office. Any doubts I may have had as to the rightness of my decision have been completely dispelled by what you've just told me."

Retief looked at her levelly. "You've been a busy girl, Miss Meuhl. Did you mention the six Terrestrials who were killed here?"

"That had no bearing on the matter of your wild behavior. I must say, in all my years in the Corps, I've never encountered a personality less suited to diplomatic work."

The screen crackled, the ten-second transmission lag having elapsed. "Mr. Retief," the face on the screen said sternly, "I am Counselor Nitworth, DSO-l, Deputy Under-Secretary for the Sector. I have received a report on your conduct, which makes it mandatory for me to relieve you administratively. Pending the findings of a Board of Inquiry, you will—"

Retief reached out and snapped off the communicator. The triumphant look faded from Miss Meuhl's face.

"Why, what is the meaning—"

"If I'd listened any longer, I might have heard something I couldn't ignore. I can't afford that, at this moment. Listen, Miss Meuhl," Retief went on earnestly, "I've found the missing cruiser. It's—"

"You heard him relieve you!"

"I heard him say he was going to, Miss Meuhl. But until I've heard and acknowledged a verbal order, it has no force. If I'm wrong, he'll get my resignation. If I'm right, that suspension would be embarrassing all around."

"You're defying lawful authority. I'm in charge here now." Miss Meuhl stepped to the local communicator.

"I'm going to report this terrible thing to the Groaci at once, and offer my profound—"

"Don't touch that screen," Retief said. "You go sit in that corner where I can keep an eye on you. I'm going to make a sealed tape for transmission to Headquarters, along with a call for an armed Task Force. Then we'll settle down to wait."

Retief, ignoring Miss Meuhl's fury, spoke into the recorder. The local communicator chimed. Miss Meuhl jumped up and stared at it.

"Go ahead," Retief said. "Answer it."

A Groacian official appeared on the screen.

"Yolanda Meuhl," he said without preamble, "for the Foreign Minister of the Groacian Autonomy, I herewith accredit you as Terrestrial Consul to Groac, in accordance with the advices transmitted to my Government direct from the Terrestrial Headquarters. As Consul, you are requested to make available for questioning Mr. J. Retief, former Consul, in connection with the assault on two Peace Keepers, and illegal entry into the offices of the Ministry of Foreign Affairs."

"Why...why," Miss Meuhl stammered. "Yes, of course, and I do want to express my deepest regrets—"

Retief rose, went to the communicator, and assisted Miss Meuhl aside.

"Listen carefully, Fith," he said. "Your bluff has been called. You don't come in and we don't come out. Your camouflage worked for nine years, but it's all over now. I suggest you keep your heads and resist the temptation to make matters worse."

"Miss Meuhl," Fith replied, "a Peace Squad waits outside your Consulate. It is clear you are in the hands of a dangerous lunatic. As always, the Groaci wish only friendship with the Terrestrials, but—"

"Don't bother," Retief cut in. "You know what was in those files I looked over this morning."

Retief turned at a sound behind him. Miss Meuhl was at the door reaching for the safe-lock release.

"Don't!" Retief jumped...too late. The door burst inward, a crowd of crested Groaci pressed into the room, pushed Miss Meuhl back, and aimed scatter guns at Retief. Police Chief Shluh pushed forward.

"Attempt no violence, Terrestrial," he said. "I cannot promise to restrain my men."

"You're violating Terrestrial territory, Shluh," Retief said steadily. "I suggest you move back out the same way you came in."

"I invited them here," Miss Meuhl spoke up. "They are here at my express wish."

"Are they? Are you sure you meant to go this far, Miss Meuhl? A squad of armed Groaci in the Consulate?"

"You are the Consul, Miss Yolanda Meuhl," Shluh said. "Would it not be best if we removed this deranged person to a place of safety?"

"Yes," Miss Meuhl said. "You're quite right, Mr. Shluh. Please escort Mr. Retief to his quarters in this building."

"I don't advise you to violate my diplomatic immunity, Fith," Retief said.

"As Chief of Mission," Miss Meuhl said quickly, "I hereby waive immunity in the case of Mr. Retief."

Shluh produced a hand recorder. "Kindly repeat your statement, madame, officially," he said. "I wish no question-

"Don't be a fool, woman," Retief said. "Don't you see what you're letting yourself in for? This would be a hell of a good time for you to figure out whose side you're on."

"I'm on the side of common decency!"

"You've been taken in. These people are concealing—"

"You think all women are fools, don't you, Mr. Retief?" She turned to the police chief and spoke into the microphone he held up.

"That's an illegal waiver," Retief said. "I'm Consul here, whatever rumors you've heard. This thing's coming out into the open, in spite of anything you can do; don't add violation of the Consulate to the list of Groacian atrocities."

"Take the man," Shluh said. Two tall Groaci came to Retief's side, guns aimed at his chest.

"Determined to hang yourselves, aren't you?" Retief said. "I hope you have sense enough not to lay a hand on this poor fool here." He jerked a thumb at Miss Meuhl. "She doesn't know anything. I hadn't had time to tell her yet. She thinks you're a band of angels."

The cop at Retief's side swung the butt of his scatter gun and connected solidly with Retief's jaw. Retief staggered against a Groacian, was caught and thrust upright, blood running down onto his shirt. Miss Meuhl yelped. Shluh barked at the guard in shrill Groacian, then turned to stare at Miss Meuhl.

"What has this man told you?"

"I—nothing. I refused to listen to his ravings."

"He said, nothing to you of…some alleged…involvement."

"I've told you." Miss Meuhl said sharply. She looked at the expressionless Groaci, then back at the blood on Retief's shirt.

"He told me nothing," she whispered. "I swear it."

"Let it lie, boys," Retief said, "before you spoil that good impression."

Shluh looked at Miss Meuhl for a long moment. Then he turned.

"Let us go," he said. He turned back to Miss Meuhl. "Do not leave this building until further advice."

"But…I am the Terrestrial Consul."

"For your safety, madam. The people are aroused at the beating of Groacian nationals by an…alien."

"So long, Meuhlsie," Retief said. "You played it real foxy."

"You'll…lock him in his quarters?" Miss Meuhl said.

"What is done with him now is a Groacian affair, Miss Meuhl. You yourself have withdrawn the protection of your government."

"I didn't mean—"

"Don't start having second thoughts," Retief said. "They can make you miserable."

"I had no choice. I had to consider the best interest of the Service."

"My mistake, I guess. I was thinking of the best interests of a Terrestrial cruiser with three hundred men aboard."

"Enough," Shluh said. "Remove this criminal." He gestured to the Peace Keepers.

"Move along," he said to Retief. He turned to Miss Meuhl. "A pleasure to deal with you, Madam."

The police car started up and pulled away. The Peace Keeper in the front seat turned to look at Retief.

"To have some sport with it, and then to kill it," he said.

"To have a fair trial first," Shluh said. The car rocked and jounced, rounded a corner, and puffed along between ornamented pastel facades.

"To have a trial and then to have a bit of sport," the Peace Keeper said.

"To suck the eggs in your own hill," Retief said. "To make another stupid mistake."

Shluh raised his short ceremonial club and cracked Retief across the head. Retief shook his head, tensed—

The Peace Keeper in the front seat beside the driver turned and rammed the barrel of his scatter gun against Retiefs ribs.

"To make no move, outworlder," he said. Shluh raised his club and carefully struck Retief again. He slumped.

The car, swaying, rounded another corner. Retief slid over against the police chief.

"To fend this animal—" Shluh began. His weak voice was cut off short as Retief's hand shot out, took him by the throat, and snapped him down onto the floor. As the guard on Retief's left lunged, Retief uppercut him, slamming his head against the door post. Retief grabbed the guard's scatter gun as it fell, and pushed it into the mandibles of the Groacian in the front seat.

"To put your pop-gun over the seat—carefully—and drop it," he said.

The driver slammed on his brakes, then whirled to raise his gun. Retief cracked a gun barrel against the head of the Groacian.

"To keep your eye-stalks on the road," he said. The driver grabbed at the tiller and shrank against the window, watching Retief with one eye, driving with another.

"To gun this thing," Retief said. "To keep moving."

Shluh stirred on the floor. Retief put a foot on him, pressing him back. The Peace Keeper beside Retief moved. Retief pushed him off the seat onto the floor. He held the scattergun with one hand and mopped at the blood on his face with the other. The car bounded over the irregular surface of the road, puffing furiously.

"Your death will not be an easy one, Terrestrial," Shluh said in Terran.

"No easier than I can help," Retief said. "Shut up for now, I want to think."

The car, passing the last of the relief-encrusted mounds, sped along between tilled fields.

"Slow down," Retief said. The driver obeyed.

"Turn down this side road."

The car bumped off onto an unpaved surface, then threaded its way back among tall stalks.

"Stop here." The car stopped, blew off steam, and sat trembling as the hot engine idled.

Retief opened the door, taking his foot off Shluh.

"Sit up," he ordered. "You two in front listen carefully." Shluh sat up, rubbing his throat.

"Three of you are getting out here. Good old Shluh is going to stick around to drive for me. If I get that nervous feeling that you're after me, I'll toss him out. That will be pretty messy, at high speed. Shluh, tell them to sit tight until dark and forget about sounding any alarms. I'd hate to see you split open and spill all over the pavement."

"To burst your throat sac, evil-smelling beast!" Shluh hissed in Groacian.

"Sorry, I haven't got one." Retief put the gun under Shluh's ear. "Tell them, Shluh; I can drive myself, in a pinch."

"To do as the foreign one says; to stay hidden until dark," Shluh said.

"Everybody out," Retief said. "And take this with you." He nudged the unconscious Groacian. "Shluh, you get in the driver's seat. You others stay where I can see you."

Retief watched as the Groaci silently followed instructions.

"All right, Shluh," Retief said softly. "Let's go. Take me to Groac Spaceport by the shortest route that doesn't go through the city, and be very careful about making any sudden movements."

Forty minutes later Shluh steered the car up to the sentry-guarded gate in the security fence surrounding the military enclosure at Groac Spaceport.

"Don't yield to any rash impulses," Retief whispered as a crested Groacian soldier came up. Shluh grated his mandibles in helpless fury.

"Drone-master Shluh, Internal Security," he croaked. The guard tilted his eyes toward Retief.

"The guest of the Autonomy," Shluh added. "To let me pass or to rot in this spot, fool?"

"To pass, Drone-master," the sentry mumbled. He was still staring at Retief as the car moved jerkily away.

"You are as good as pegged-out on the hill in the pleasure pits now, Terrestrial," Shluh said in Terran. "Why do you venture here?"

"Pull over there in the shadow of the tower and stop," Retief said.

Shluh complied. Retief studied a row of four slender ships silhouetted against the early dawn colors of the sky.

"Which of those boats are ready to lift?" Retief demanded.

Shluh swiveled a choleric eye.

"All of them are shuttles; they have no range. They will not help you."

"To answer the question, Shluh, or to get another crack on the head."

"You are not like other Terrestrials, you are a mad dog."

"We'll rough out a character sketch of me later. Are they fueled up? You know the procedures here. Did those shuttles just get in, or is that the ready line?"

"Yes. All are fueled and ready for take-off."

"I hope you're right, Shluh. You and I are going to drive over and get in one; if it doesn't lift, I'll kill you and try the next one. Let's go."

"You are mad. I have told you: these boats have not more than ten thousand ton-seconds capacity; they are useful only for satellite runs."

"Never mind the details. Let's try the first in line."

Shluh let in the clutch and the steam car clanked and heaved, rolling off toward the line of boats.

"Not the first in line," Shluh said suddenly. "The last is the most likely to be fueled. But—"

"Smart grasshopper," Retief said. "Pull up to the entry port, hop out, and go right up. I'll be right behind you."

"The gangway guard. The challenging of—"

"More details. Just give him a dirty look and say what's necessary. You know the technique."

The car passed under the stem of the first boat, then the second. There was no alarm. It rounded the third and shuddered to a stop by the open port of the last vessel.

"Out," Retief said. "To make it snappy."

Shluh stepped from the car, hesitated as the guard came to attention, then hissed at him and mounted the steps. The guard looked wonderingly at Retief, mandibles slack.

"An outworlder!" he said. He unlimbered his scatter gun. "To stop here, meat-faced one."

Up ahead, Shluh turned.

"To snap to attention, litter-mate of drones." Retief rasped in Groacian. The guard jumped, waved his eye stalks, and came to attention.

"About face!" Retief hissed. "To hell out of here—march!"

The guard tramped off across the ramp. Retief took the steps two at a time, slammed the port shut behind himself.

"I'm glad your boys have a little discipline, Shluh," Retief said. "What did you say to him?"

"I but—"

"Never mind. We're in. Get up to the control compartment."

"What do you know of Groacian Naval vessels?"

"Plenty. This is a straight copy from the life boat you lads hijacked. I can run it. Get going."

Retief followed Shluh up the companionway into the cramped control room.

"Tie in, Shluh," Retief ordered.

"This is insane. We have only fuel enough for a one-way transit to the satellite; we cannot enter orbit, nor can we land again! To lift this boat is death. Release me. I promise you immunity."

"If I have to tie you in myself, I might bend your head in the process."

Shluh crawled onto the couch, and strapped in.

"Give it up," he said. "I will see that you are re-instated—with honor. I will guarantee a safe-conduct—"

"Count-down," Retief said. He threw in the autopilot.

"It is death!" Shluh screeched.

The gyros hummed, timers ticked, relays closed. Retief lay relaxed on the acceleration pad. Shluh breathed noisily, his mandibles clicking rapidly.

"That I had fled in time," he said in a hoarse whisper. "This is not a good death."

"No death is a good death," Retief said, "not for a while yet." The red light flashed on in the center of the panel, and sound roared out into the breaking day. The ship trembled, then lifted. Retief could hear Shluh's whimpering even through the roar of the drive.

"Perihelion," Shluh said dully. "To begin now the long fall back."

"Not quite," Retief said. "I figure eighty-five seconds to go." He scanned the instruments, frowning.

"We will not reach the surface, of course," Shluh said. "the pips on the screen are missiles. We have a rendezvous in space, Retief. In your madness, may you be content."

"They're fifteen minutes behind us, Shluh. Your defenses are sluggish."

"Nevermore to burrow in the grey sands of Groac," Shluh mourned.

Retief's eyes were fixed on a dial face.

"Any time now," he said softly. Shluh canted his eye stalks.

"What do you seek?"

Retief stiffened. "Look at the screen," he said. Shluh looked. A glowing point, off-center, moving rapidly across the grid...

"What—?"

"Later—"

Shluh watched as Retiefs eyes darted from one needle to another.

"How..."

"For your own neck's sake, Shluh, you'd better hope this works." He flipped the sending key.

"2396 TR-42 G, this is the Terrestrial Consul at Groac, aboard Groac 902, vectoring on you at an MP fix of 91/54/942. Can you read me? Over."

"What forlorn gesture is this?" Shluh whispered. "You cry in the night to emptiness."

"Button your mandibles," Retief snapped, listening. There was a faint hum of stellar background noise. Retief repeated his call.

"Maybe they hear but can't answer," he muttered. He flipped the key.

"2396, you've got forty seconds to lock a tractor beam on me, before I shoot past you."

"To call into the void," said Shluh. "To—"

"Look at the DV screen."

Shluh twisted his head and looked. Against the background mist of stars, a shape loomed, dark and inert.

"It is...a ship," he said, "a monster ship..."

"That's her," Retief said. "Nine years and a few months out of New Terra on a routine mapping mission; the missing cruiser, *IVS Terrific.*"

"Impossible," Shluh hissed. "The hulk swings in a deep cometary orbit."

"Right, and now it's making its close swing past Groac."

"You think to match orbits with the derelict? Without power? Our meeting will be a violent one, if that is your intent."

"We won't hit; we'll make our pass at about five thousand yards.

"To what end, Terrestrial? You have found your lost ship; what then? Is this glimpse worth the death we die?"

"Maybe they're not dead," Retief said.

"Not dead?" Shluh lapsed into Groacian. "To have died in the burrow of one's youth. To have burst my throat sac before I embarked with a mad alien to call up the dead."

"2396, make it snappy," Retief called. The speaker crackled heedlessly. The dark image on the screen drifted past, dwindling now.

"Nine years, and the mad one speaking as to friends," Shluh raved. "Nine years dead, and still to seek them."

"Another ten seconds," Retief said softly, "and we're out of range. Look alive, boys."

"Was this your plan, Retief?" Shluh reverted to Terran. "Did you flee Groac and risk all on this slender thread?"

"How long would I have lasted in a Groaci prison?"

"Long and long, my Retief," Shluh hissed, "under the blade of an artist."

Abruptly the ship trembled, seemed to drag, rolling the two passengers in their couches. Shluh hissed as the restraining harness cut into him. The shuttle boat was pivoting heavily, up-ending. Crushing acceleration forces built. Shluh gasped, crying out shrilly.

"What...is...it...?"

"It looks," said Retief, "like we've had a little bit of luck."

"On our second pass," the gaunt-faced officer said, "they let fly with something. I don't know how it got past our screens. It socked home in the stem and put the main pipe off the air. I threw full power to the emergency shields, and broadcast our identification on a scatter that should have hit every receiver within a parsec; nothing. Then the transmitter blew. I was a fool to send the boat down, but I couldn't believe, somehow..."

"In a way it's lucky you did, captain. That was my only lead."

"They tried to finish us after that. But, with full power to the screens, nothing they had could get through. Then they called on us to surrender."

Retief nodded. "I take it you weren't tempted?"

"More than you know. It was a long swing out on our first circuit. Then coming back in, we figured we'd hit. As a last resort I would have pulled back power from the screens and tried to adjust the orbit with the steering jets, but the bombardment was pretty heavy. I don't think we'd have made it. Then we swung past and headed out again. We've got a three-year period. Don't think I didn't consider throwing in the towel."

"Why didn't you?"

"The information we have is important. We've got plenty of stores aboard, enough for another ten years, if necessary. Sooner or later I knew a Corps search vessel would find us."

Retief cleared his throat. "I'm glad you stuck with it, Captain. Even a backwater world like Groac can kill a lot of people when it runs amok."

"What I didn't know," the captain went on, "was that we're not in a stable orbit. We're going to graze atmosphere pretty deeply this pass, and in another sixty days we'd be back to stay. I guess the Groaci would be ready for us."

"No wonder they were sitting on this so tight. They were almost in the clear."

"And you're here now," the captain said. "Nine years, and we weren't forgotten. I knew we could count on—"

"It's over now, captain. That's what counts."

"Home… After nine years…"

"I'd like to take a look at the films you mentioned," Retief said. "The ones showing the installations on the satellite."

The captain complied. Retief watched as the scene unrolled, showing the bleak surface of the tiny moon as the *Terrific* had seen it, nine years before. In harsh black and white, row on row of identical hulls cast long shadows across the pitted metallic surface of the satellite.

"They had quite a little surprise planned; your visit must have panicked them," Retief said.

"They should be about ready to go, by now. Nine years…"

"Hold that picture," Retief said suddenly. "What's that ragged black line across the plain there?"

"I think it's a fissure. The crystalline structure—"

"I've got what may be an idea," Retief said. "I had a look at some classified files last night, at the Foreign Office. One was a progress report on a fissionable stock-pile. It didn't make much sense at the time. Now I get the picture. Which is the north end of that crevasse?"

"At the top of the picture."

"Unless I'm badly mistaken, that's the bomb dump. The Groaci like to tuck things underground. I wonder what a direct hit with a 50 megaton missile would do to it?"

"If that's an ordnance storage dump," the captain said, "it's an experiment I'd like to try."

"Can you hit it?"

"I've got fifty heavy missiles aboard. If I fire them in direct sequence, it should saturate the defenses. Yes, I can hit it."

"The range isn't too great?"

"These are the deluxe models." The captain smiled balefully. "Video guidance. We could steer them into a bar and park 'em on a stool."

"What do you say we try it?"

"I've been wanting a solid target for a long time," the captain said.

Half an hour later, Retief propelled Shluh into a seat before the screen.

"That expanding dust cloud used to be the satellite of Groac, Shluh," he said. "Looks like something happened to it."

The police chief stared at the picture.

"Too bad," Retief said. "But then it wasn't of any importance, was it, Shluh?"

Shluh muttered incomprehensibly.

Just a bare hunk of iron, Shluh, as the Foreign Office assured me when I asked for information."

"I wish you'd keep your prisoner out of sight," the captain said. "I have a hard time keeping my hands off him."

"Shluh wants to help, captain. He's been a bad boy and I have a feeling he'd like to co-operate with us now, especially in view of the eminent arrival of a Terrestrial ship, and the dust cloud out there," Retief said.

"What do you mean?"

"Captain, you can ride it out for another week, contact the ship when it arrives, get a tow in, and your troubles are over. When your films are shown in the proper quarter, a Peace Force will come out here and reduce Groac to a sub-technical cultural level and set up a monitor system to insure she doesn't get any more expansionist ideas—not that she can do much now, with her handy iron mine in the sky gone."

"That's right, and—"

"On the other hand, there's what I might call the diplomatic approach…"

He explained at length. The captain looked at him thoughtfully.

"I'll go along," he said. "What about this fellow?"

Retief turned to Shluh. The Groacian shuddered, retracting his eye stalks.

"I will do it," he said faintly.

"Right," Retief said. "Captain, if you'll have your men bring in the transmitter from the shuttle, I'll place a call to a fellow named Fith at the Foreign Office." He turned to Shluh. "And when I get him, Shluh, you'll do everything exactly as I've told you—or have Terrestrial monitors dictating in Groac City."

"Quite candidly, Retief," Counselor Nitworth said, "I'm rather nonplussed. Mr. Fith of the Foreign Office seemed almost painfully lavish in your praise. He seems most eager to please you. In the light of some of the evidence I've turned up of highly irregular behavior on your part, it's difficult to understand."

"Fith and I have been through a lot together," Retief said. "We understand each other."

"You have no cause for complacency, Retief," Nitworth said. "Miss Meuhl was quite justified in reporting your case. Of course, had she known that you were assisting Mr. Fith in his marvelous work, she would have modified her report somewhat, no doubt. You should have confided in her."

"Fith wanted to keep it secret, in case it didn't work out. You know how it is."

"Of course. And as soon as Miss Meuhl recovers from her nervous breakdown, there'll be a nice promotion awaiting her. The girl more than deserves it for her years of unswerving devotion to Corps policy."

"Unswerving," Retief said. "I'll go along with that."

"As well you may, Retief. You've not acquitted yourself well in this assignment. I'm arranging for a transfer; you've alienated too many of the local people."

"But as you said, Fith speaks highly of me…"

"True. It's the cultural intelligentsia I'm referring to Miss Meuhl's records show that you deliberately affronted a number of influential groups by boycotting—"

"Tone deaf," Retief said. "To me a Groacian blowing a nose-whistle sounds like a Groacian blowing a nose-whistle."

"You have to come to terms with local aesthetic values. Learn to know the people as they really are. It's apparent from some of the remarks Miss Meuhl quoted in her report that you held the Groaci in rather low esteem. But how wrong you were. All the while they were working unceasingly to rescue those brave lads marooned aboard our cruiser. They pressed on, even after we ourselves had abandoned the search. And when they discovered that it had been a collision with their satellite, which disabled the craft, they made that magnificent gesture—unprecedented. One hundred thousand credits in gold to each crew member, as a token of Groacian sympathy."

"A handsome gesture," Retief murmured.

"I hope, Retief, that you've learned from this incident. In view of the helpful part you played in advising Mr. Fith in matters of procedure to assist in his search, I'm not recommending a reduction in grade. We'll overlook the affair, give you a clean slate. But in the future, I'll be watching you closely."

"You can't win 'em all," Retief said.

"You'd better pack up; you'll be coming along with us in the morning." Nitworth shuffled his papers together. "I'm sorry that I can't file a more flattering report on you. I would have liked to recommend your promotion, along with Miss Meuhl's."

"That's okay," Retief said. "I have my memories."

...Ofttimes, the expertise displayed by experienced Terrestrial Chiefs of Mission in the analysis of local political currents enabled these dedicated senior officers to secure acceptance of Corps commercial programs under seemingly insurmountable conditions of adversity. Ambassador Crodfoller's virtuoso performance in the reconciliation of rival elements at Petreac added new lustre to Corps prestige...
Vol VIII, reel 8. 489 A. E. (AD 2950)

PALACE REVOLUTION

RETIEF PAUSED before a tall mirror to check the overlap of the four sets of lapels that ornamented the vermilion cutaway of a First Secretary and Consul.

"Come along, Retief," Magnan said. "The ambassador has a word to say to the staff before we go in."

"I hope he isn't going to change the spontaneous speech he plans to make when the Potentate impulsively suggests a trade agreement along the lines they've been discussing for the last two months."

"Your derisive attitude is uncalled for, Retief," Magnan said sharply. "I think you realize it's delayed your promotion in the Corps."

Retief took a last glance in the mirror. "I'm not sure I want a promotion. It would mean more lapels."

Ambassador Crodfoller pursed his lips, waiting until Retief and Magnan took places in the ring of Terrestrial diplomats around him.

"A word of caution only, gentlemen. Keep always foremost in your minds the necessity for our identification with the Nenni Caste. Even a hint of familiarity with lower echelons could mean the failure of the mission. Let us remember: the Nenni represent authority here on Petreac; their traditions must be observed, whatever our personal preferences. Let's go along now; the Potentate will be making his entrance any moment."

Magnan came to Retief's side as they moved toward the salon.

"The ambassador's remarks were addressed chiefly to you, Retief," he said. "Your laxness in these matters is notorious. Naturally, I believe firmly in democratic principles myself."

"Have you ever had a feeling, Mr. Magnan, that there's a lot going on here that we don't know about?"

Magnan nodded. "Quite so; Ambassador Crodfoller's point exactly. Matters which are not of concern to the Nenni are of no concern to us."

"Another feeling I get is that the Nenni aren't very bright. Now suppose—"

"I'm not given to suppositions, Retief. We're here to implement the policies of the Chief of Mission. And I should dislike to be in the shoes of a member of the Staff whose conduct jeopardized the agreement that's to be concluded here tonight."

A bearer with a tray of drinks rounded a fluted column, shied as he confronted the diplomats, fumbled the tray, grabbed, and sent a glass crashing to the floor. Magnan leaped back, slapping at the purple cloth of his pants leg. Retief's hand shot out and steadied the tray. The servant rolled his terrified eyes.

"I'll take one of those, now that you're here," Retief said easily, lifting a glass from the tray. "No harm done. Mr. Magnan's just warming up for the big dance."

A Nenni major-domo bustled up, rubbing his hands politely.

"Some trouble here? What happened, Honorables, what, what..."

"The blundering idiot," Magnan spluttered. "How dare—"

"You're quite an actor, Mr. Magnan," Retief said. "If I didn't know about your democratic principles, I'd think you were really angry."

The servant ducked his head and scuttled away.

"Has this fellow given dissatisfaction...?" The majordomo eyed the retreating bearer.

"I dropped my glass," Retief said. "Mr. Magnan's upset because he hates to see liquor wasted."

Retief turned and found himself face-to-face with Ambassador Crodfoller.

"I witnessed that," the ambassador hissed. "By the goodness of Providence the Potentate and his retinue haven't appeared yet, but I can assure you the servants saw it. A more un-Nenni-like display I would find it difficult to imagine."

Retief arranged his features in an expression of deep interest. "More un-Nenni-like, sir? I'm not sure I—"

"Bah!" The ambassador glared at Retief. "Your reputation has preceded you, sir. Your name is associated with a number of the most bizarre incidents in Corps history. I'm warning you; I'll tolerate nothing." He turned and stalked away.

"Ambassador-baiting is a dangerous sport, Retief," Magnan said.

Retief took a swallow of his drink. "Still, it's better than no sport at all."

"Your time would be better spent observing the Nenni mannerisms; frankly, Retief, you're not fitting into the group at all well."

"I'll be candid with you, Mr. Magnan; the group gives me the willies."

"Oh, the Nenni are a trifle frivolous, I'll concede. But it's with them that we must deal. And you'd be making a contribution to the overall mission if you abandoned that rather arrogant manner of yours." Magnan looked at Retief critically. "You can't help your height, of course, but couldn't you curve your back just a bit—and possibly assume a more placating expression? Just act a little more..."

"Girlish?"

"Exactly." Magnan nodded, then looked sharply at Retief.

Retief drained his glass and put it on a passing tray.

"I'm better at acting girlish when I'm well juiced," he said. "But I can't face another sorghum and soda. I suppose it would be un-Nenni-like to slip one of the servants a credit and ask for a Scotch and water."

"Decidedly." Magnan glanced toward a sound across the room.

"Ah, here's the Potentate now..." He hurried off.

Retief watched the bearers coming and going, bringing trays laden with drinks, carrying off empties. There was a lull in the drinking now, as the diplomats gathered around the periwigged chief of state and his courtiers. Bearers loitered near the service door, eyeing the notables. Retief strolled over to the service door and pushed through it into a narrow white-tiled hall filled with kitchen odors. Silent servants gaped as he passed and watched him as he moved along to the kitchen door and stepped inside.

A dozen or more low-caste Petreacans, gathered around a long table in the center of the room, looked up, startled. A heap of long-bladed bread knives, carving knives and cleavers lay in the center of the table. Other knives were thrust into belts or held, in the hands of the men. A fat man in the yellow sarong of a cook stood frozen in the act of handing a twelve-inch cheese-knife to a tall one-eyed sweeper.

Retief took one glance, then let his eyes wander to a far corner of the room. Humming a careless little tune, he sauntered across to the open liquor shelves, selected a garish green bottle, then turned unhurriedly back toward the door. The group of servants watched him, transfixed.

As Retief reached the door, it swung inward. Magnan stood in the doorway, looking at him.

"I had a premonition," he said.

"I'll bet it was a dandy. You must tell me all about it in the salon."

"We'll have this out right here," Magnan snapped. "I've warned you—" His voice trailed off as he took in the scene around the table.

"After you," Retief said, nudging Magnan toward the door. "What's going on here?" Magnan barked. He stared at the men and started around Retief. A hand stopped him.

"Let's be going," Retief said, propelling Magnan toward the hall.

"Those knives!" Magnan yelped. "Take your hands off me, Retief! What are you men—"

Retief glanced back. The fat cook gestured suddenly, and the men faded back. The cook stood, arm cocked, a knife across his palm.

"Close the door and make no sound," he said softly.

Magnan pressed back against Retief. "Let's...r-run..." he faltered.

Retief turned slowly, put his hands up.

"I don't run very well with a knife in my back," he said. "Stand very still, Mr. Magnan, and do just what he tells you."

"Take them out through the back," the cook said.

"What does he mean," Magnan spluttered. "Here, you—"

"Silence," the cook said, almost casually. Magnan gaped at him, then closed his mouth.

Two of the men with knives came to Retief's side, gestured, grinning broadly.

"Let's go, peacocks," said one.

Retief and Magnan silently crossed the kitchen, went out the back door, stopped on command, and stood waiting. The sky was brilliant with stars and a gentle breeze stirred the tree-tops beyond the garden. Behind them the servants talked in low voices.

"You go too, Illy," the cook was saying. "Do it here," said another.

"And carry them down?"

"Pitch 'em behind the hedge."

"I said the river. Three of you is plenty for a couple of Nenni dandies."

"They're foreigners, not Nenni. We don't know—"

"So they're foreign Nenni. Makes no difference. I've seen them. I need every man here; now get going."

"What about the big guy?"

"Him? He waltzed into the room and didn't notice a thing. But watch the other one."

At a prod from a knife point, Retief moved off down the walk, two of the escort behind him and Magnan, another going ahead to scout the way.

Magnan moved closer to Retief.

"Say," he said in a whisper, "that fellow in the lead—isn't he the one who spilled the drink? The one you took the blame for?"

"That's him, all right. He doesn't seem nervous any more, I notice."

"You saved him from serious punishment," Magnan said, "He'll be grateful; he'll let us go…"

"Better check with the fellows with the knives before you act on that."

"Say something to him," Magnan hissed, "remind him."

The lead man fell back in line with Retief and Magnan.

"These two are scared of you," he said, grinning and jerking a thumb toward the knife-handlers. "They haven't worked around the Nenni like me; they don't know you."

"Don't you recognize this gentleman?" Magnan said, "He's—"

"He did me a favor," the man said. "I remember."

"What's it all about?" Retief asked.

"The revolution. We're taking over now."

"Who's 'we'?"

"The People's Anti-Fascist Freedom League."

"What are all the knives for?"

"For the Nenni; and for you foreigners."

"What do you mean?" gasped Magnan.

"We'll slit all the throats at one time; saves a lot of running around."

"When will that be?"

"Just at dawn—and dawn comes early, this time of year. By full daylight the PAFFL will be in charge."

"You'll never succeed," Magnan said. "A few servants with knives; you'll all be caught and executed."

"By who; the Nenni?" The man laughed, "You Nenni are a caution."

"But we're not Nenni—"

"We've watched you; you're the same. You're part of the same blood-sucking class."

"There are better ways," Magnan said. "This killing won't help you. I'll personally see to it that your grievances are heard in the Corps Courts. I can assure you that the plight of the down-trodden workers will be alleviated. Equal rights for all."

"Threats won't help you," the man said. "You don't scare me."

"Threats? I'm promising relief to the exploited classes of Petreac."

"You must be nuts. You trying to upset the system or something?"

"Isn't that the purpose of your revolution?"

"Look, Nenni, we're tired of you Nenni getting all the graft. We want our turn. What good it do us to run Petreac if there's no loot?"

"You mean you intend to oppress the people? But they're your own group."

"Group, schmoop. We're taking all the chances; we're doing the work. We deserve the pay-off. You think we're throwing up good jobs for the fun of it?"

"You're basing a revolt on these cynical premises?"

"Wise up, Nenni; there's never been a revolution for any other reason."

"Who's in charge of this?" Retief said. "Shoke, the head chef."

"I mean the big boss; who tells Shoke what to do?"

"Oh, that's Zorn. Look out, here's where we start down the slope. It's slippery."

"Look," Magnan said. "You. This—"

"My name's Illy."

"Mr. Illy, this man showed you mercy when he could have had you beaten."

"Keep moving. Yeah, I said I was grateful."

"Yes," Magnan said, swallowing hard. "A noble emotion, gratitude."

"I always try to pay back a good turn," Illy said. "Watch your step now on this sea-wall."

"You'll never regret it."

"This is far enough." Illy motioned to one of the knife men. "Give me your knife, Vug."

The man passed his knife to Illy. There was an odor of sea-mud and kelp. Small waves slapped against the stones of the sea wall. The wind was stronger here.

"I know a neat stroke," Illy said. "Practically painless. Who's first?"

"What do you mean?" Magnan quavered.

"I said I was grateful; I'll do it myself, give you a nice clean job. You know these amateurs: botch it up and have a guy floppin' around, yellin' and spatterin' everybody up."

"I'm first," Retief said. He pushed past Magnan, stopped suddenly, and drove a straight punch at Illy's mouth.

The long blade flicked harmlessly over Retief's shoulder as Illy fell. Retief took the unarmed servant by the throat and belt, lifted him, and slammed him against the third man. Both screamed as they tumbled from the sea-wall into the water with a mighty splash. Retief turned back to Illy, pulled off the man's belt, and strapped his hands together.

Magnan found his voice. "You...we...they..."

"I know."

"We've got to get back," Magnan said. "Warn them."

"We'd never get through the rebel cordon around the palace. And if we did, trying to give an alarm would only set the assassinations off early."

"We can't just..."

"We've got to go to the source: this fellow Zorn. Get him to call it off."

"We'd be killed. At least we're safe here."

Illy groaned and opened his eyes. He sat up.

"On your feet, Illy," Retief said.

Illy looked around. "I'm sick."

"The damp air is bad for you. Let's be going." Retief pulled the man to his feet. "Where does Zorn stay when he's in town?"

"What happened? Where's Vug and..."

"They had an accident. Fell in the pond."

Illy gazed down at the restless black water.

"I guess I had you Nenni figured wrong."

"We Nenni have hidden qualities. Let's get moving before Vug and Slug make it to shore and start it all over again."

"No hurry," Illy said. "They can't swim." He spat into the water. "So long, Vug. So long, Toscin. Take a pull at the Hell Horn for me." He started off along the sea wall toward the sound of the surf.

"You want to see Zorn, I'll take you see Zorn. I can't swim either."

"I take it," Retief said, "that the casino is a front for his political activities."

"He makes plenty off it. This PAFFL is a new kick. I never heard about it until maybe a couple months ago."

Retief motioned toward a dark shed with an open door.

"We'll stop here," he said, "long enough to strip the gadgets off these uniforms."

Illy, hands strapped behind his back, stood by and watched as Retief and Magnan removed medals, ribbons, orders, and insignia from the formal diplomatic garments.

"This may help some," Retief said, "if the word is out that two diplomats are loose."

"It's a breeze," Illy said. "We see cats in purple and orange tailcoats all the time."

"I hope you're right," Retief said. "But if we're called, you'll be the first to go, Illy."

"You're a funny kind of Nenni," Illy said, eyeing Retief. "Toscin and Vug must be wonderin' what happened to 'em."

"If you think I'm good at drowning people, you ought to see me with a knife. Let's get going."

"It's only a little way now. But you better untie me. Somebody's liable to notice it and start askin' questions and get me killed."

"I'll take the chance. How do we get to the casino?"

"We follow this street. When we get to the Drunkard's Stairs we go up and it's right in front of us. A pink front with a sign like a big luck wheel."

"Give me your belt, Magnan," Retief said.

Magnan handed it over.

"Lie down, Illy."

The servant looked at Retief.

"Vug and Toscin will be glad to see me. But they'll never believe me." He lay down. Retief strapped his feet together and stuffed a handkerchief in his mouth.

"Why are you doing that?" Magnan asked. "We need him."

"We know the way now and we don't need anyone to announce our arrival." Magnan looked at the man. "Maybe you'd better—ah, cut his throat."

Illy rolled his eyes.

"That's a very un-Nenni-like suggestion, Mr. Magnan," Retief said. "But if we have any trouble finding the casino following his directions, I'll give it serious thought."

There were few people in the narrow street. Shops were shuttered, windows dark.

"Maybe they heard about the coup," Magnan said. "They're lying low."

"More likely they're at the palace checking out knives."

They rounded a corner, stepped over a man curled in the gutter snoring heavily, and found themselves at the foot of a long flight of littered stone steps.

"The Drunkard's Stairs are plainly marked," Magnan sniffed.

"I hear sounds up there...sounds of merrymaking."

"Maybe we'd better go back."

"Merrymaking doesn't scare me. Come to think of it, I don't know what the word means." Retief started up, Magnan behind him.

At the top of the long stair a dense throng milled in the alley-like street.

A giant illuminated roulette wheel revolved slowly above them. A loud-speaker blared the chant of the croupiers from the tables inside. Magnan and Retief moved through the crowd toward the wide-open doors.

Magnan plucked at Retief's sleeve. "Are you sure we ought to push right in like this? Maybe we ought to wait a bit, look around."

"When you're where you have no business being," Retief said, "always stride along purposefully. If you loiter, people begin to get curious."

Inside, a mob packed the wide low-ceilinged room and clustered around gambling devices in the form of towers, tables, and basins.

"What do we do now?" Magnan asked.

"We gamble. How much money do you have in your pockets?"

"Why...a few credits..." Magnan handed the money to Retief. "But what about the man Zorn?"

"A purple cutaway is conspicuous enough, without ignoring the tables. We'll get to Zorn in due course."

"Your pleasure, gents," a bullet-headed man said, eyeing the colorful evening clothes of the diplomats. "You'll be wantin' to try your luck at the Zoop tower, I'd guess. A game for real sporting gents."

"Why...ah..." Magnan said.

"What's a Zoop tower?" Retief asked.

"Out-of-towners, hey?" The bullet-headed man shifted his dope-stick to the other corner of his mouth. "Zoop is a great little game. Two teams of players buy into the pot; each player takes a lever; the object is to make the ball drop from the top of the tower into your net. Okay?"

"What's the ante?"

"I got a hundred-credit pot workin' now, gents."

Retief nodded. "We'll try it."

The shill led the way to an eight-foot tower mounted on gimbals. Two perspiring men in trade-class pullovers gripped two of the levers that controlled the tilt of the tower. A white ball lay in a hollow in the thick glass platform at the top. From the center an intricate pattern of grooves led out to the edge of the glass. Retief and Magnan took chairs before the two free levers.

"When the light goes on, gents, work the lever to jack the tower. You got three gears; takes a good arm to work top gear. That's this button here. The little little knob controls what way you're goin'. May the best team win. I'll take the hundred credits now."

Retief handed over the money. A red light flashed on, and Retief tried the lever. It moved easily, with a ratcheting sound. The tower trembled, slowly tilted toward the two perspiring workmen pumping frantically at their levers. Magnan started slowly, accelerating as he saw the direction the tower was taking.

"Faster, Retief," he said. "They're winning."

"This is against the clock, gents," the bullet-headed man said. "If nobody wins when the light goes off, the house takes all."

"Crank it over to the left," Retief said.

"I'm getting tired."

"Shift to a lower gear."

The tower leaned. The ball stirred and rolled into a concentric channel. Retief shifted to middle gear and worked the lever. The tower, creaking to a stop, started back upright.

"There isn't any lower gear," Magnan gasped. One of the two on the other side of the, tower shifted to middle gear; the other followed suit. They worked harder now, heaving against the stiff levers. The tower quivered, then moved slowly toward their side.

"I'm exhausted," Magnan gasped. Dropping the lever, he lolled back in the chair, gulping air. Retief, shifting position, took Magnan's lever with his left hand.

"Shift it to middle gear," he said. Magnan gulped, punched the button and slumped back, panting.

"My arm," he said. "I've injured myself."

The two men in pullovers conferred hurriedly as they cranked their levers; then one punched a button, and the other reached across, using his left arm to help.

"They've shifted to high," Magnan said. "Give up, it's hopeless."

"Shift me to high. Both buttons."

Magnan complied. Retief's shoulders bulged. He brought one lever down, then the other, alternately, slowly at first, then faster. The tower jerked, tilted toward him, farther... The ball rolled in the channel, found an outlet—

Abruptly, both Retief's levers froze. The tower trembled, wavered, and moved back. Retief heaved. One lever folded at the base, bent down, and snapped off short. Retief braced his feet, gripped the other lever with both hands and pulled. There was a squeal of metal, a loud twang. The lever came free, a length of broken cable flopping into view. The tower fell over as the two on the other side scrambled aside.

"Hey!" the croupier yelled, appearing from the crowd. "You wrecked my equipment!"

Retief got up and faced him.

"Does Zorn know you've got your tower rigged for suckers?"

"You tryin' to call me a cheat?"

The crowd had fallen back, ringing the two men. The croupier glanced around. With a lightning motion he pulled out a knife.

"That'll be five hundred credits for the equipment," he said. "Nobody calls Kippy a cheat."

Retief picked up the broken lever.

"Don't make me hit you with this, Kippy."

Kippy looked at the bar.

"Comin' in here," he said indignantly, looking to the crowd for support, "bustin' up my rig, threatenin' me…"

"I want a hundred credits," Retief said. "Now."

"Highway robbery!" Kippy yelled.

"Better pay up," somebody said.

"Hit him, mister," another in the crowd yelled.

A broad-shouldered man with greying hair pushed through the crowd and looked around. "You heard him, Kippy. Give."

The shill growled, tucked his knife away, reluctantly peeled a bill from a fat roll and handed it over.

The newcomer looked from Retief to Magnan.

"Pick another game, strangers," he said. "Kippy made a little mistake."

"This is small-time stuff," Retief said. "I'm interested in something big."

The broad-shouldered man lit a perfumed dope stick, then sniffed at it.

"What would you call big?" he said softly.

"What's the biggest you've got?"

The man narrowed his eyes, smiling. "Maybe you'd like to try Slam."

"Tell me about it."

"Over here." The crowd opened up and made a path. Retief and Magnan followed across the room to a brightly-lit glass-walled box. There was an arm-sized opening at waist height, and inside was a hand grip. A four-foot clear plastic globe a quarter full of chips hung in the center. Apparatus was mounted at the top of the box.

"Slam pays good odds," the man said. "You can go as high as you like. Chips cost you a hundred credits. You start it up by dropping a chip in here." He indicated a slot.

"You take the hand grip. When you squeeze, it unlocks and starts to turn. Takes a pretty good grip to start the globe turning. You can see, it's full of chips. There's a hole at the top. As long as you hold the grip, the bowl turns. The harder you squeeze, the faster it turns. Eventually it'll turn over to where the hole is down, and chips fall out. If you let up and the bowl stops, you're all through.

"Just to make it interesting, there's contact plates spotted around the bowl; when one of 'em lines up with a live contact, you get a little jolt-guaranteed non-lethal. But if you let go, you lose. All you've got to do is hold on long enough, and you'll get the pay-off."

"How often does this random pattern put the hole down?"

"Anywhere from three minutes to fifteen, with the average grip. Oh, by the way, one more thing. That lead block up there..." The man motioned with his head toward a one-foot cube suspended by a thick cable. "It's rigged to drop every now and then: averages five minutes. A warning light flashes first. You can set the clock back on it by dropping another chip—or you can let go the grip. Or you can take a chance; sometime's the light's a bluff."

Retief looked at the massive block of metal.

"That would mess up a man's dealing hand, wouldn't it?"

"The last two jokers who were too cheap to feed the machine had to have 'em off; their arm, I. mean. That lead's heavy stuff."

"I don't suppose your machine has a habit of getting stuck, like Kippy's?"

The broad-shouldered man frowned.

"You're a stranger," he said. "You don't know any better."

"It's a fair game, mister," someone called.

"Where do I buy the chips?"

The man smiled. "I'll fix you up. How many?"

"One."

"A big spender, eh?" The man snickered and handed over a large plastic chip.

Retief stepped to the machine and dropped the coin.

"If you want to change your mind," the man said, "you can back out now. All it'll cost you is the chip you dropped."

Retief, reaching through the hole, took the grip. It was leather-padded, hand-filling. He squeezed it. There was a click and bright lights sprang up. The globe began to twirl lazily. The four-inch hole at its top was plainly visible.

"If ever the hole gets in position, it will empty very quickly," Magnan said.

Suddenly, a brilliant white light flooded the glass cage. A sound went up from the spectators.

"Quick, drop a chip," someone yelled. "You've only got ten seconds..."

"Let go!" Magnan pleaded.

Retief sat silent, holding the grip, frowning up at the weight. The globe twirled faster now. Then the bright white light winked off.

"A bluff!" Magnan gasped.

"That's risky, stranger," the grey-templed man said.

The globe was turning rapidly now, oscillating from side to side. The hole seemed to travel in a wavering loop, dipping lower, swinging up high, then down again.

"It has to move to the bottom soon," Magnan said. "Slow it down, so it doesn't shoot past."

"The slower it goes, the longer it takes to get to the bottom," someone said.

There was a crackle, and Retief stiffened. Magnan heard a sharp intake of breath. The globe slowed, and Retief shook his head, blinking.

The broad-shouldered man glanced at a meter.

"You took pretty near a full jolt, that time," he said.

The hole in the globe was tracing an oblique course now, swinging to the center, then below.

"A little longer," Magnan said.

"That's the best speed I ever seen on the Slam ball," someone said. "How much longer can he hold it?"

Magnan looked at Retief's knuckles. They showed white against the grip. The globe tilted farther, swung around, then down; two chips fell out, clattered down a chute and into a box.

"We're ahead," Magnan said. "Let's quit."

Retief shook his head. The globe rotated, dipped again; three chips fell.

"She's ready," someone called.

"It's bound to hit soon," another voice added excitedly. "Come on, mister!"

"Slow down," Magnan said. "So it won't move past too quickly."

"Speed it up, before that lead block gets you," someone called.

The hole swung high, over the top, then down the side. Chips rained out, six, eight...

"Next pass," a voice called.

The white warning light flooded the cage. The globe whirled; the hole slid over the top, down down...a chip fell, two more...

Retief half rose, clamped his jaw, and crushed the grip. Sparks flew, and the globe slowed, chips spewing. It stopped and swung back. Weighted by the mass of chips at the bottom, it stopped again with the hole centered. Chips cascaded down the chute, filled the box and spilled on the floor. The crowd yelled.

Retief released the grip and withdrew his arm at the same instant that the lead block slammed down.

"Good lord," Magnan said. "I felt that through the floor."

Retief turned to the broad-shouldered man.

"This game's all right for beginners," he said. "But I'd like to talk a really big gamble. Why don't we go to your office, Mr. Zorn?"

"Your proposition interests me," Zorn said, an hour later. "But there's some angles to this I haven't mentioned yet."

"You're a gambler, Zorn, not a suicide," Retief said. "Take what I've offered. Your dream of revolution was fancier, I agree, but it won't work."

"How do I know you birds aren't lying?" Zorn snarled. He stood up and strode up and down the room. "You walk in here and tell me I'll have a squadron of Corps Peace Enforcers on my neck, that the Corps won't recognize my regime. Maybe you're right; but I've got other contacts. They say different." Whirling, he stared at Retief.

"I have pretty good assurance that once I put it over, the Corps will have to recognize me as the legal de facto government of Petreac. They won't meddle in internal affairs."

"Nonsense," Magnan spoke up, "the Corps will never deal with a pack of criminals calling themselves—"

"Watch your language, you!" Zorn rasped.

"I'll admit Mr. Magnan's point is a little weak," Retief said. "But you're overlooking something. You plan to murder a dozen or so officers of the Corps Diplomatique Terrestrienne along with the local wheels. The Corps won't overlook that. It can't."

"Their tough luck they're in the middle," Zorn muttered.

"Our offer is extremely generous, Mr. Zorn," Magnan said. "The post you'll get will pay you very well indeed; as against certain failure of your coup, the choice should be simple."

Zorn eyed Magnan. "I thought you diplomats weren't the type to go around making deals under the table. Offering me a job—it sounds phony as hell."

"It's time you knew," Retief said. "There's no phonier business in the galaxy than diplomacy."

"You'd better take it, Mr. Zorn," Magnan said.

"Don't push me," Zorn said. "You two walk into my headquarters empty-handed and big-mouthed. I don't know what I'm talking to you for. The answer is no. N-i-x, no!"

"Who are you afraid of?" Retief said softly.

Zorn glared at him.

"Where do you get that 'afraid' routine? I'm top man here. What have I got to be afraid of?"

"Don't kid around, Zorn. Somebody's got you under his thumb. I can see you squirming from here."

"What if I let your boys alone?" Zorn said suddenly. "The Corps won't have anything to say then, huh?"

"The Corps has plans for Petreac, Zorn. You aren't part of them. A revolution right now isn't part of them. Having the Potentate and the whole Nenni caste slaughtered isn't part of them. Do I make myself clear?"

"Listen," Zorn said urgently, "I'll tell you guys a few things. You ever heard of a world they call Rotune?"

"Certainly," Magnan said. "It's a near neighbor of yours, another backward—that is, emergent."

"Okay," Zorn said. "You guys think I'm a piker, do you? Well, let me wise you up. The Federal Junta on Rotune is backing my play. I'll be recognized by Rotune, and the Rotune fleet will stand by in case I need any help. I'll present the CDT with what you call a *fait accompli*."

"What does Rotune get out of this? I thought they were your traditional enemies."

"Don't get me wrong. I've got no use for Rotune; but our interests happen to coincide right now."

"Do they?" Retief smiled grimly. "You can spot a sucker as soon as he comes through that door out there—but you go for a deal like this."

"What do you mean?" Zorn looked angrily at Retief. "It's fool-proof."

"After you get in power, you'll be fast friends with Rotune, is that it?"

"Friends, hell. Just give me time to get set, and I'll square a few things with that-"

"Exactly. And what do you suppose they have in mind for you?"

"What are you getting at?"

"Why is Rotune interested in your take-over?"

Zorn studied Retief's face. "I'll tell you why," he said. "It's you birds; you and your trade agreement. You're here to tie Petreac into some kind of trade combine. That cuts Rotune out. They don't like that. And anyway, we're doing all right out here; we don't need any commitments to a lot of fancy-pants on the other side of the galaxy."

"That's what Rotune has sold you, eh?" Retief said, smiling.

"Sold, nothing." Zorn ground out his dope stick then lit another. He snorted angrily.

"Okay—what's your idea?"

"You know what Petreac is getting in the way of imports as a result of the trade agreement?"

"Sure, a lot of junk. Clothes washers, tape projectors, all that kind of stuff."

"To be specific," Retief said, "there'll be 50,000 Tatone B-3 dry washers; 100,000 Glo-float motile lamps; 100,000 Earth Worm Minor garden cultivators; 25,000 Veco space heaters; and 75,000 replacement elements for Ford Monomeg drives."

"Like I said: a lot of junk," Zorn said.

Retief leaned back, looking sardonically at Zorn. "Here's the gimmick, Zorn," he said. "The Corps is getting tired of Petreac and Rotune carrying on their two-penny war out here. Your privateers have a nasty habit of picking on innocent bystanders. After studying both sides, the Corps has decided Petreac would be a little easier to do business with; so this trade agreement was worked out. The Corps can't openly sponsor an arms shipment to a belligerent; but personal appliances are another story."

"So what do we do—plow 'em under with back-yard cultivators?" Zorn looked puzzled. "What's the point?"

"You take the sealed monitor unit from the washer, the repeller field generator from the lamp, the converter control from the cultivator, etc., etc. You fit these together according to some very simple instructions; presto! you have one hundred thousand Standard-class Y hand blasters; just the thing to turn the tide in a stalemated war fought with obsolete arms."

"Good Lord," Magnan said. "Retief, are you—"

"I have to tell him. He has to know what he's putting his neck into."

"Weapons, hey?" Zorn said. "And Rotune knows about it...?"

"Sure they know about it; it's not too hard to figure out. And there's more. They want the CDT delegation included in the massacre for a reason; it will put Petreac out of the picture; the trade agreement will go to Rotune; and you and your new regime will find yourselves looking down the muzzles of your own blasters."

Zorn threw his dope-stick to the floor with a snarl.

"I should have smelled something when that Rotune agent made his pitch." Zorn looked at the clock on the wall.

"I've got two hundred armed men in the palace. We've got forty minutes to get over there before the rocket goes up."

In the shadows of the palace terrace, Zorn turned to Retief. "You'd better stay here out of the way until I've spread the word. Just in case."

"Let me caution you against any...ah...slip-ups, Mr. Zorn," Magnan said. "The Nenni are not to be molested."

Zorn looked at Retief. "Your friend talks too much. I'll keep my end of it; he'd better keep his."

"Nothing's happened yet, you're sure?" Magnan said.

"I'm sure," Zorn said. "Ten minutes to go; plenty of time."

"I'll just step into the salon to assure myself that all is well," Magnan said.

"Suit yourself. Just stay clear of the kitchen, or you'll get your throat cut." Zorn sniffed at his dope-stick. "I sent the word for Shoke," he muttered. "Wonder what's keeping him?"

Magnan stepped to a tall glass door, eased it open, and poked his head through the heavy draperies. As he moved to draw back, a voice was faintly audible. Magnan paused, his head still through the drapes.

"What's going on there?" Zorn rasped. He and Retief stepped up behind Magnan.

"…breath of air," Magnan was saying.

"Well, come along, Magnan!" Ambassador Crodfoller's voice snapped.

Magnan shifted from one foot to the other, then pushed through the drapes.

"Where've you been, Mr. Magnan?" The ambassador's voice was sharp.

"Oh…ah…a slight accident, Mr. Ambassador."

"What's happened to your shoes? Where are your insignia and decorations?"

"I—ah—spilled a drink on them. Maybe I'd better nip up to my room and slip into some fresh medals."

The ambassador snorted. "A professional diplomat never shows his liquor, Magnan. It's one of his primary professional skills. I'll speak to you about this later. I had expected your attendance at the signing ceremony, but under the circumstances I'll dispense with that. You'd better depart quietly through the kitchen."

"The kitchen? But it's crowded…I mean…"

"A little loss of caste won't hurt at this point, Mr. Magnan. Now kindly move along before you attract attention. The agreement isn't signed yet."

"The agreement…" Magnan babbled, sparring for time, "very clever, Mr. Ambassador. A very neat solution."

The sound of an orchestra came up suddenly, blaring a fanfare.

Zorn shifted restlessly, his ear against the glass. "What's your friend pulling?" he rasped. "I don't like this."

"Keep cool, Zorn. Mr. Magnan is doing a little emergency salvage on his career."

The music died away with a clatter.

"…my God." Ambassador Crodfoller's voice was faint. "Magnan, you'll be knighted for this. Thank God you reached me. Thank God it's not too late. I'll find some excuse. I'll get, off a gram at once."

"But you— "

"It's all right, Magnan. You were in time. Another ten minutes and the agreement would have been signed and transmitted. The wheels would have been put in motion. My career would have been ruined…"

Retief felt a prod at his back. He turned.

"Double-crossed," Zorn said softly. "So much for the word of a diplomat."

Retief looked at the short-barreled needler in Zorn's hand.

"I see you hedge your bets, Zorn."

"We'll wait here until the excitement's over inside. I wouldn't want to attract any attention right now."

"Your politics are still lousy, Zorn. The picture hasn't changed. Your coup hasn't got a chance."

"Skip it. I'll take up one problem at a time."

"Magnan's mouth has a habit of falling open at the wrong time."

"That's my good luck I heard it. So there'll be no agreement, no guns, no fat job for Tammany Zorn, hey? Well, I can still play it the other way. What have I got to lose?"

With a lightning quick movement, Retief's hand chopped down across Zorn's wrist. The needler clattered to the ground as Retief's hand clamped on Zorn's arm, whirling him around.

"In answer to your last question," Retief said, "your neck."

"You haven't got a chance, double-crosser," Zorn gasped. "Shoke will be here in a minute. Tell him it's all off."

"Twist harder, mister. Break it off at the shoulder. I'm telling him nothing."

"The kidding's over, Zorn. Call it off or I'll kill you."

"I believe you. But you won't have long to remember it."

"All the killing will be for nothing. You'll be dead and the Rotunes will step into the power vacuum."

"So what? When I die, the world ends."

"Suppose I make you another offer, Zorn?"

"Why would it be any better than the last one?"

Retief released Zorn's arm, pushed him away, stooped and picked up the needler.

"I could kill you, Zorn; you know that."

"Go ahead."

Retief reversed the needler and held it out.

"I'm a gambler too, Zorn. I'm gambling you'll listen to what I have to say."

Zorn snatched the gun and stepped back. He looked at Retief. "That wasn't the smartest bet you ever made, but go ahead. You've got maybe ten seconds."

"Nobody double-crossed you, Zorn. Magnan put his foot in it; too bad. Is that a reason to kill yourself and a lot of other people who've bet their lives on you?"

"They gambled and lost. Tough."

"Maybe they haven't lost yet—if you don't quit."

"Get to the point."

Retief spoke earnestly for a minute and a half. Zorn stood, gun aimed, listening. Then both men turned as footsteps approached along the terrace. A fat man in a yellow sarong padded up to Zorn.

Zorn tucked the needler in his waistband.

"Hold everything, Shoke," he said. "Tell the boys to put the knives away; spread the word fast: it's all off."

"I want to commend you, Retief," Ambassador Crodfoller said expansively. "You mixed very well at last night's affair; actually, I was hardly aware of your presence."

"I've been studying Mr. Magnan's work," Retief said.

"A good man, Magnan. In a crowd, he's virtually invisible."

"He knows when to disappear, all right."

"This has been in many ways a model operation, Retief." The ambassador patted his paunch contentedly. "By observing local social customs and blending harmoniously with the court, I've succeeded in establishing a fine, friendly, working relationship with the Potentate."

"I understand the agreement has been put off a few days."

The Ambassador chuckled. "The Potentate's a crafty one. Through...ah...a special study I have been conducting, I learned last night that he had hoped to, shall I say, 'put one over' on the Corps."

"Great Heavens," Retief said.

"Naturally, this placed me in a difficult position. It was my task to quash this gambit, without giving any indication that I was aware of its existence."

"A hairy position indeed."

"Quite casually, I informed the Potentate that certain items which had been included in the terms of the agreement had been deleted and others substituted. I admired him at that moment, Retief. He took it coolly—appearing completely indifferent—perfectly dissembling his very serious disappointment. Of course, he could hardly do otherwise without in effect admitting his plot."

"I noticed him dancing with three girls each wearing a bunch of grapes; he's very agile for a man of his bulk."

"You mustn't discount the Potentate. Remember, beneath that mask of frivolity, he had absorbed a bitter blow."

"He had me fooled," Retief said.

"Don't feel badly; I confess at first I, too, failed to sense his shrewdness." The ambassador nodded and moved off along the corridor.

Retief turned and went into an office. Magnan looked up from his desk.

"Ah, Retief," he said. "I've been meaning to ask you. About the...ah...blasters; are you—"

Retief leaned on Magnan's desk and looked at him. "I thought that was to be our little secret."

"Well, naturally I—" Magnan closed his mouth and swallowed. "How is it, Retief," he said sharply, "that you were aware of this blaster business, when the ambassador himself wasn't?"

"Easy," Retief said. "I made it up."

"You what!" Magnan looked wild. "But the agreement— it's been revised. Ambassador Crodfoller has gone on record."

"Too bad. Glad I didn't tell him about it."

Magnan leaned back and closed his eyes.

"It was big of you to take all the…blame," Retief said, "when the ambassador was talking about knighting people."

Magnan opened his eyes. "What about that gambler, Zorn? Won't he be upset when he learns the agreement is off? After all, I…that is, we, or you, had more or less promised him—"

"It's all right. I made another arrangement. The business about making blasters out of common components wasn't completely imaginary. You can actually do it, using parts from an old-fashioned disposal unit."

"What good will that do him?" Magnan whispered, looking nervous. "We're not shipping in any old-fashioned disposal units."

"We don't need to. They're already installed in the palace kitchen—and in a few thousand other places, Zorn tells me."

"If this ever leaks…" Magnan put a hand to his forehead.

"I have his word on it that the Nenni slaughter is out. This place is ripe for a change; maybe Zorn is what it needs."

"But how can we know?" Magnan said. "How can we be sure?"

"We can't. But it's not up to the Corps to meddle in Petreac's internal affairs." He leaned over, picked up Magnan's desk lighter, and lit a cigar. He blew a cloud of smoke toward the ceiling.

"Right?" he said.

Magnan looked at him and nodded weakly. "Right."

"I'd better be getting along to my desk," Retief said. "Now that the ambassador feels that I'm settling down at last."

"Retief," Magnan said, "tonight, I implore you: stay out of the kitchen—no matter what."

Retief raised his eyebrows.

"I know," Magnan said. "If you hadn't interfered, we'd all have had our throats cut. But at least…" He paused. "we'd have died in accordance with regulations."

THE END

If you've enjoyed this book, you will not want to miss these terrific titles…

ARMCHAIR SCI-FI, FANTASY, & HORROR DOUBLE NOVELS, $12.95 each

D-21   **EMPIRE OF EVIL** by Robert Arnette
      THE SIGN OF THE TIGER by Alan E. Nourse & J. A. Meyer

D-22   **OPERATION SQUARE PEG** by Frank Belknap Long
      ENCHANTRESS OF VENUS by Leigh Brackett

D-23   **THE LIFE WATCH** by Lester Del Rey
      CREATURES OF THE ABYSS by Murray Leinster

D-24   **LEGION OF LAZARUS** by Edmond Hamilton
      STAR HUNTER by Andre Norton

D-25   **EMPIRE OF WOMEN** by John Fletcher
      ONE OF OUR CITIES IS MISSING by Irving Cox

D-26   **THE WRONG SIDE OF PARADISE** by Raymond F. Jones
      THE INVOLUNTARY IMMORTALS by Rog Phillips

D-27   **EARTH QUARTER** by Damon Knight
      ENVOY TO NEW WORLDS by Keith Laumer

D-28   **SLAVES TO THE METAL HORDE** by Milton Lesser
      HUNTERS OUT OF TIME by Joseph E. Kelleam

D-29   **RX JUPITER SAVE US** by Ward Moore
      BEWARE THE USURPERS by Geoff St. Reynard

D-30   **SECRET OF THE SERPENT** by Don Wilcox
      CRUSADE ACROSS THE VOID by Dwight V. Swain

ARMCHAIR SCIENCE FICTION CLASSICS, $12.95 each

C-7   **THE SHAVER MYSTERY, pt. 1**
      by Richard S. Shaver

C-8   **THE SHAVER MYSTERY, pt. 2**
      by Richard S. Shaver

C-9   **MURDER IN SPACE**
      by David V. Reed

ARMCHAIR MASTERS OF SCIENCE FICTION SERIES, $16.95 each

M-3   **MASTERS OF SCIENCE FICTION, Vol. Three**
Robert   Sheckley, "The Perfect Woman" and other stories

M-4   **MASTERS OF SCIENCE FICTION, Vol. Four**
      Mack Reynolds, part one, "Stowaway" and other stories